You Had Me at Chocolate

You Had Me at Chocolate

A Marietta Chocolate Wars Romance

Amy Andrews

You Had Me at Chocolate
Copyright© 2021 Amy Andrews
Tule Publishing First Printing, November 2021

The Tule Publishing, Inc.

ALL RIGHTS RESERVED

First Publication by Tule Publishing 2021

Cover design by Llewellen Designs

No part of this book may be used or reproduced in any manner whatsoever without written permission except in the case of brief quotations embodied in critical articles and reviews.

This is a work of fiction. Names, characters, places, and incidents are products of the author's imagination or are used fictitiously. Any resemblance to actual events, locales, organizations, or persons, living or dead, is entirely coincidental.

ISBN: 978-1-956387-55-1

Dedication

For my brother, Phillip. I wish things could have
been different.

Chapter One

IT HADN'T SEEMED like a particularly big deal to Jude Barlow, at the age of twelve, to pinkie promise to a marriage with fellow twelve-year-old Clem—Clementine—Jones if neither of them had found *the one* by the age of thirty. Marriage was a reasonably unsavory prospect given the terrible state of his parents' union but, as thirty had seemed ancient and Clem had such pretty eyes and smiled a lot, it had been too far away to worry about.

And, even at twelve, Clem had possessed that quality that made a person believe everything would be okay, which had been sorely lacking in his life.

Sure, they only ever saw each other once a year at summer camp but *her* parents never seemed like they were only one argument away from a divorce so, she clearly knew what she was talking about. Except now he was approaching her house in Marietta, Montana—unannounced—with an origami crane in one hand and an engagement ring in the other, it *was* a big deal.

A big, fucking, hairy, bodacious deal.

Idiotic, some might say, but then he was severely jet-lagged after his four-day trek from the barren beauty of central Africa to the jagged peaks and big sky of Montana.

1

And, a promise was a promise. Despite the non-legally binding nature of the pinkie swear.

Plus… he needed her. Her sensible, rational calm. Her fondness for lists and planning. Her down-to-earth, girl next door-ness. Because he was done with a procession of parties and the revolving door of women who liked to go to parties. Who liked designer dresses, and flashy jewels, and getting their pictures taken. He was done with vanity. Theirs *and* his.

What he needed was Clem. Good, solid, dependable, book-nerd, Clem.

A real nip pervaded the night air on this last day in September as he took in her neat, low-set clapboard house on Third Street through gritty eyes. The low buzz of chatter, muffled laughter, and the background hum of music drifted out as he stood at the gate. There was obviously a party going on. Her *birthday* party he presumed given today was her big three-zero.

That had always been a possibility, of course, and he hesitated for a second. Maybe he should go back to the Graff and get some much-needed sleep? Maybe she wouldn't want him to gate-crash her big night? But maybe, she was secretly waiting for him to come through the door and fulfil that promise from all those years ago?

Women liked grand gestures, right?

Mind—such as it currently was—made up, he opened the gate, ignoring the way his heart rate sped up as he strode down the path. This whole thing might be a little under-thought, but he wanted it suddenly with a desperate kind of intensity.

The laughter was louder as he took the two stairs to the porch and, before he could talk himself out of it, knocked on the door twice—loudly. He was about to knock a third time when it opened to reveal a woman with an ice-blonde bob, blunt bangs sitting just above eyebrow height, and a champagne glass in her hand. The house behind was crowded with people, the volume of their chatter and the music increasing considerably now the door was open.

"Lordy," she said with a slight slur, looking him up and down and, evidently, finding much to be happy about, "please tell me someone ordered a strip-o-gram and you're it."

Jude blinked. Strippers did birthday parties in buttfuck Montana? "I'm afraid not."

She sighed. "I didn't think I could get that lucky." Taking a sip of her champagne, her eyes narrowed. "Wait." Jude steeled himself for the inevitable. "Oh my god." She poked him in the chest. "You're that *Yes, Chef* guy. Jude someone…"

He gave a small smile. Not even a year tucked away in sub-Sahara Africa and looking like hell after his tournament of travel, had dimmed his celebrity. "Barlow," he supplied.

"Well." She leaned her shoulder into the doorframe. "I take that back. This *is* my lucky night. Who needs a stripper when Jude Barlow is at the door?"

Jude laughed warily as he glanced over her shoulder at the partygoers, his palm sweating around the small, robin's-egg blue box. "I'm assuming the birthday girl's around somewhere?"

The woman narrowed her eyes again. "How do you

3

know Clem?"

"We're old friends." When the woman crossed her arms like she had all the time in the world to stay right where she was, he elaborated. "We met in summer camp in third grade."

She cocked an eyebrow, the tidbit sparking obvious interest. "*Really?* She never mentioned that to me."

"It was a long time ago," he dismissed. Because it had been. Although, had he been less exhausted, he might have been slightly miffed that she hadn't bragged about him—even just a little.

"Did you bring a gift?" she asked, her slur making her sound a little belligerent.

He did if he was allowed to count the two-carat, princess-cut diamond ring he'd purchased on whim at the Tiffany store in Charles De Gaulle airport. Although, knowing Clementine, she'd probably go more gaga over the origami crane. "Yes."

"Good." The woman nodded. "She's out back, follow me."

She turned then with a swish of her long purple skirt and Jude followed. Barely any one looked at him as he passed, engrossed as they were in their conversations and that suited him just fine. He wasn't tired anymore—he was nervous. Old Jude would have scoffed at the feeling, considered it a weakness instead of a normal reaction to uncertain events. The fact he hadn't been nervous in a lot of years gave him hope that his attempts to reset the clock, to get his life back in balance, hadn't been in vain.

The thud of his heart echoed in his ears obliterating the

country music playing in the background as they approached the open back door and it was a relief to step out into the night after purple skirt. Jude inhaled the cooler air, his body too warm, his clothes too tight. His palm, closed around the box, was too damn sweaty.

He was really going to do this.

Purple skirt led him past groups of partygoers that had spilled out into the yard toward the glow of a fire blazing from a raised metal pit. People were huddled around it, drinking and laughing and chatting as his guide elbowed her way through the circle.

"Hey, Clem, visitor for you."

Jude took a deep, cleansing breath as he, too, elbowed his way in to find her turning, her entire body gilded in light, an orange halo emblazoning the tips of her dark, springy curls. The breath he'd taken stilled somewhere between his throat and his lungs as the impact of seeing her again after all this time walloped him straight in the center of his chest. He hadn't seen her since he was twelve but those years fell away and, in this moment, it was like they'd never parted.

She was still short and cute, her big amber eyes still glowed despite the light behind throwing her face into shadow, her chipmunk cheeks were still rosy. But she was *definitely* grown-up and wearing the hell out of a pair of skinny jeans and a sparkling top that shimmered like a disco ball thanks to the dance of the fire.

The girl next door was gone. Goodbye Clem, hello Clementine.

A frown drew her brows together as she walked closer and he held his breath again until her forehead smoothed out and a smile lifted the corners of her mouth. "Oh my god, *Jude?*" She grinned. "Is that you?"

Finding his breath for a second time, Jude grinned also—he couldn't help it, she still had a very pretty smile. "It is."

She practically levitated the rest of the way and was in his arms in the blink of an eye. There was no formality or shyness as she raised herself up on her tippy toes and landed a smacker on his cheek before linking her arms around his neck and pressing her forehead into the hollow of his throat.

It felt good. *So* fucking good. Her body aligned with his, her curls tickling his chin, her perfume weaving around him like a spell. How long had it been since a woman had hugged him out of sheer joy? Because she'd missed him?

How long had it been since a woman had hugged him without an agenda?

"You remembered my birthday," she said as she eased back from him, seemingly oblivious to the curious glances from every single person in the backyard.

"How could I forget? It's a day after mine."

"That's right," she said. "We're so old now!"

"The big three-zero." Or one hundred in jet-lag years. "It's all downhill from here, apparently."

"Or maybe it's just beginning?" she suggested, a teasing twinkle sparking in the syrupy-gold of her eyes.

Jude's heartbeat spiked. Was she thinking about their pinkie-swear pact? Warmth flushed through his system at the thought. "Here." He presented her with the origami he'd practically crushed in his sweaty hand. "For you."

She eased away from him as she took it, her lips gently

YOU HAD ME AT CHOCOLATE

parting as her fingertips caressed the folded wings. Glancing at him, she smiled and he swore he could see her eyes misting over. "Did you actually finally learn how to do this or did you buy it already made?"

There was still a tease in her voice but it was husky now and it wrapped around him, around them, drawing them into a warm, intimate bubble—just the two of them. The nostalgia of an idyllic yesteryear reached right inside Jude's chest and cradled his heart. "It was all me."

He'd found a pad of origami sheets in an airport shop on his way to Africa which had triggered a memory of Clementine. He hadn't thought about her in a long time so he'd bought it on a whim. And there hadn't been a lot to do at night...

The intimate mood was broken very quickly, however, by purple skirt's belligerent, "You got her a paper crane?" She was clearly unimpressed. "*That's* your birthday present?"

"No." Jude slid his eyes sideways taking in a very disapproving glower. "There's more."

To prove it, he took a step back and knelt down on one knee.

A collective gasp ran around every person witnessing the unfolding events, which dragged Clem's attention from the origami to Jude. Her smile faded.

"Clem... Clementine." Jude's voice almost cracked and he cleared his throat as he tried to zone out the fascinated-horrified gawkers in his peripheral vision. "At the age of twelve you made me pinkie swear that we would get married if we were both still single at thirty and—" Jude cleared his throat again. "Here we are."

7

He didn't miss her frown as he unfurled his hand to reveal the Tiffany ring box. Nor did he miss the murmur that ran around the gathering.

"Jude?" She stared at him intently. "What are you doing?"

He opened the lid to reveal the ring and this time there were *gasps* as the firelight did its job, reflecting on the exquisitely cut facets, making it twinkle more brilliantly than the stars overhead.

"Oh. My. God." Purple skirt gaped as she pressed her hand to her chest.

"I'm asking you to marry me, Clementine. I know we haven't seen each other in a long time but I think we knew even back then that we'd make a good team and I know it seems a little... crazy but, I think we should do it." He pushed the box across the small space separating them until it was only an inch from the tips of her fingers. "What do you say?"

For long moments, she did nothing, *said* nothing. Nobody said or did anything. The hush that had fallen over the yard was absolute. Even the party noise from inside seemed to fade as everyone stared at Clementine and waited. Jude's pulse, though, was *loud*. It raced like a train, hurtling against his sternum, rattling along his ribs, and echoing through his ears.

When Clementine finally moved it was only a blink but that blink said a lot. That blink said *everything*.

It was a very loud blink.

"Let's talk inside, shall we?" she said, through stiff lips. Then, turning on her heel, she marched through the stunned onlookers in the direction of the door.

Purple skirt winced at him as Jude rose to his feet feeling every one of those transit hours. He ignored her—he ignored all of them—as he, too, turned, and followed Clementine into the house.

BY THE TIME Clem had pushed through all her friends, who wanted a quick hug or chat with the birthday girl to the relative quiet of her bedroom, she was reeling. She left the door open knowing Jude was somewhere behind but pleased to have a moment alone. Time to think. To try and understand why a guy she hadn't seen since she was *twelve* had just asked her to marry him in front of one hundred and twenty Marietta locals.

Thank god her parents had gone home twenty minutes ago. Her mother had been despairing about her lack of grandchildren for several years now—something like this could give her very bad ideas. And Clem didn't think for a minute the fact Jude was a relative stranger would matter to her mother.

Trina Jones wanted to be a me-maw *bad*.

It had been cold outside and Clem had been grateful for the fire but now her cheeks were flaming and her body was melting. Great, her first hot flash. At *thirty*.

God, maybe it really was all downhill from here?

"Hey."

She glanced up from the origami crane she'd been absently staring at to find him in the doorway and, for a second, she forgot he'd just proposed to her with a giant freaking diamond ring, and was swept up in just how *nicely* he'd matured. As a twelve-year-old he'd been a gangly redhead with freckles, ears that stuck out, and a goofy kind of smile.

He wasn't gangly now.

Nope, Jude had filled out *well*. She'd seen him on the TV, of course, keeping track of his meteoric rise to fame from afar. But there'd been makeup and camera angles and he'd been younger then. Clean-cut. Frozen in that stage between boy and man. *Arrogant* though—so sure of himself, the latest culinary sensation thanks to the incredible reach of the worldwide phenomenon that was *Yes, Chef!*

This guy was older—a little rougher around the edges. A lot more *un*sure of himself.

His red hair was darker too—more chestnut than rust— and his freckles had faded or were hidden behind the whiskery growth on his jawline. There were crow's feet around his eyes, which she didn't think was from excessive smiling.

No, combined with that cragginess to his complexion, Clem figured it was more to do with time spent outdoors. Which, given he'd disappeared a year ago, to do humanitarian work in Africa according to his mother's Christmas card, would fit. Clem hadn't thought much about it at the time other than to hope he was finding whatever he was looking for after his abrupt decision to sell his very successful New York restaurant and drop out of sight.

Except he wasn't in Africa now. He was in her house. Asking her to marry him. For the love of all that was holy…

"Come in. Shut the door." She didn't want an audience.

YOU HAD ME AT CHOCOLATE

He did as he was told, entering the room to about half-way, in an easy long-legged stride. Dark blue jeans sat snug on his hips, hanging in a way that emphasised without clinging—very designer. His ribbed khaki Henley stretched nicely over broad shoulders and flat abs.

He hadn't had *them* at twelve.

"You look great, Clementine."

His face warmed into a slow smile, his voice oozing over her like warm honey. Clem blinked. He hadn't had that voice at twelve, either.

"Are you drunk?" she demanded, launching straight into her attack, even more annoyed at him now her body was taking total leave of its senses.

"What?" He frowned. "No."

"High?"

He stiffened. "Contrary to tabloid opinion, I *do not* do drugs."

"Were you recently dropped on your head?"

Sighing, he took a step forward, stopping abruptly when she shook her head violently at him. "Clementine."

He never used to call her Clementine, either. Always Clem. Just like everyone else—except for her mother who used it whenever her daughter displeased her. Which seemed to be all the time, lately. And if she hadn't been pissed at him and his ridiculous... *stunt*, right now, she might even have admitted to liking it. Liking how grown-up it felt. How it made her feel like a woman, not the *girl* she'd been back when they'd known each other better.

But she *was* pissed. Very, very pissed.

"No, seriously, you must have some kind of head injury,

because I cannot for the life of me think why you would pull that crap out there in front of almost every damn person I know in this town."

"Well… I am a little jet-lagged."

Which went further to explaining some of the crow's feet. But not the turning up out of nowhere and publicly proposing thing. "So this is what?" she demanded. "A severe case of narcolepsy?"

"Okay." He held his hands up in a placatory manner like he was trying to calm a fractious child. "You're upset."

Clementine's vision turned a deep scarlet red as her pissed-off hit the stratosphere. "Don't you dare patronise me," she hissed and he took a step back.

"Sorry, I—"

"I am not *upset*," she growled with a kind of demonic possession nobody, including herself, would ever have associated with Clem Jones, mild-mannered librarian. "I am fucking furious!"

It was his turn to blink. To look completely shocked.

"What?" she demanded, irritated by his apparent surprise.

"I just… the Clementine I knew never cussed."

The deep scarlet turned to thick red mist as the blood vessels at her temples throbbed in unison. So, *this* was how it felt to blow a cerebral aneurysm.

"The Clementine you knew was twelve years old! My mother would have washed my mouth out with soap if I'd have dared to use a cuss word."

She would have heard Clem say it too—even with three hundred miles separating summer camp from Marietta.

Trina Jones had eyes in the back of her head and ears like a bat.

That had been bitten by a radioactive spider.

He chuckled for a moment but, obviously reading the room and Clem's lack of amusement, the smile slipped from his face. "Yeah, I guess you're all grown-up now, huh."

His gaze dropped briefly. It wasn't lecherous or sleezy; just took her in before returning to her face, but Clem's belly did a weird kind of wobble. She ordered it to stop—no weird wobbles allowed around Jude. Her childhood *friend*. Who had *never* given her the belly wobbles. Even when she'd hatched that ridiculous juvenile marriage-pact scheme, he hadn't given her the belly wobbles.

But he'd been funny and smart and he'd had a plan in life. He'd wanted to run a little inn like the one his family stayed at every year in Texas when his father went bird watching—whooping cranes to be precise—in the Aransas National Wildlife Refuge. And why she remembered that detail, Clem had no idea. Probably because she'd always thought it was kinda interesting.

Different. Something her librarian brain had appreciated.

She also remembered he'd wanted to make the best apple cobbler in the world for his guests just as the woman who owned the inn had made for her guests and that kind of detail had been attractive to an eight-year-old Clem on the day they'd first met. Her plans to become a librarian had been in full swing at that stage, so she'd admired similar dedication.

What better attribute could she have asked for in a husband? She came from a long line of planners, after all. Her father was a *town planner*. That was what the Jones family did—they planned. And she'd been pretty damn smug about accomplishing all she'd set out to achieve.

Until recently. Until her midlife crisis. Her very inconvenient midlife crisis.

About a year ago, Sondra, a librarian friend of hers from college, had landed a job at the Met in New York and suddenly this life Clem had set out for herself had left her feeling... wanting. In an effort to establish her career and cement her place in the Marietta library hierarchy, she'd become predictable.

Boring.

And, in her usual style, she'd taken steps to fix it. It hadn't been her desire to throw a hand grenade into her life—she loved living in Marietta, she loved small-town life, she loved being a librarian in her small town—but she *had* wanted to shake it up.

A little.

So, she'd ditched the guy she'd been seeing on and off for three years who'd been more friend than lover—Reuben had been as *un*-heartbroken as her—and booked a six-week European Contiki tour. Which had been *ah*-mazing and made her want to travel more but her job didn't allow for that kind of time off on a regular basis. She'd been trying to figure out how to have both when another friend of hers from Livingstone had been diagnosed with breast cancer—at thirty.

Clem had been shaken to the core. Macey was in remission now and doing fine but the whole experience had made Clem realize how short life was. How it was passing her by.

YOU HAD ME AT CHOCOLATE

And suddenly, a hand grenade hadn't seemed like such a bad idea.

A hand grenade an associate of Sondra's—Eliza Redgold from New York—had thrown Clem's way two months ago. And Clem had gleefully pulled the pin.

The last thing she'd expected was a different kind of blast—one from her past—presenting her with a Tiffany rock and a marriage proposal. Out of the blue. *Not* because he was declaring undying love but because they'd promised each other at *twelve*. Love, passion, excitement apparently didn't enter into the equation.

Even had Clem *not* decided her life would take a direction that didn't involve a romantic relationship—for a good few years anyway—his proposal wasn't exactly appealing.

"I *am* all grown-up," she said testily. "And so are you. What the hell are you thinking?"

He sighed a weary sigh as he shoved a hand through the short, shaggy layers of his chestnut hair that already looked like they'd been finger combed *plenty*. They covered his prominent ears, too, she realized. Or maybe he'd just grown into them?

The action drew her eyes to the flex of a perfectly proportioned bicep bunching in the confines of his sleeve. He sure hadn't had *biceps* at twelve.

"I'm sorry. I'm kinda wrecked and it's been a while and I'll be the first to admit that I'm rusty where women are concerned but I know they like grand gestures so I figured… go big or go home, right?"

"Man." Clem shook her head. "You really *are* rusty, aren't you?"

"I've been in Africa."

Like that explained it. "I know. Your mom said in her Christmas card."

"To be honest, I don't know if I ever knew what women want."

"Well let me clue you in. *This* woman doesn't like being put on the spot."

He rubbed his chin, his whiskers making a scratchy sound that traveled straight to her nipples, which was disconcerting to say the least. Clem thanked the universe for the disguise of her sparkly top.

"Okay." He nodded. "Noted. But... we made a pact, Clementine."

She blinked. *Again.* Yeah, she remembered the pact. Had actually remembered it this morning when she'd woken. It had brought a wry smile to her mouth and she'd moved on. "We. Were. *Twelve.*"

"I know it sounds... a bit ludicrous—"

"A bit?" More like freaking crazy. The damn man was giving her eyelids epilepsy.

"But..." He shrugged, plainly ignoring her shrill outburst. "We're old friends. You're single, I'm single. That's not nothing."

It wasn't *something* though, was it? It wasn't fireworks and giddiness and a crazy leap in the pulse. Just because Clem was about to embark on a whole new stage of her life and wasn't, therefore, in the market for a relationship right now, didn't mean she didn't want the whole enchilada when/if she did decide to say yes to a man bearing a rock.

"How do you know I'm single?" Clem demanded because there *had* been belly wobbles and she didn't want to think about where they fit on the giddiness-leaping pulse spectrum.

"Your Christmas card said you were."

Clem gaped at him. Was he for real? "That was *nine* months ago. I could have had a damn baby in nine months. You don't think I could have got myself another boyfriend in that time?"

"Of course." His brow scrunched as he held out both hands in what she assumed was supposed to be a calming gesture. "You just never seemed the type—"

"The *type?*" she interrupted, the sinister note in her voice as loud as the rush of blood through her head.

"Wait, no." He did the hand calming movement again. "I'm really screwing this all up. I didn't mean it like that. I mean the type to act that fast. It took you two weeks during that first camp for you to decide which Jonas brother you liked the best. You had a diary with columns of pros and cons for each of them."

Heat rose to Clem's cheeks remembering how she'd agonized over that particularly pressing dilemma.

"I just mean," he said, his voice gentle, "you were always very... considered."

Oh dear god. She'd *always* been boring, hadn't she? *Even at eight.*

But—wait. Did a boring person get tipsy on cheap prosecco in Rome and almost get arrested for dancing in the Trevi Fountain at three in the morning? Did a boring person sunbathe topless in Majorca—in October? Did a boring person kiss not one, not two, but three different men in six weeks across a dozen European countries?

Not exactly outrageous behavior for a Contiki tour, granted, but it had been revolutionary for Clem.

"Who knows?" Jude interrupted her thinking. "Maybe our twelve-year-old selves knew something that we didn't know about ourselves?"

Clem rolled her eyes. He could not be serious about this. "We made a tweenie marriage pact. I think that tells you a *lot* about how *little* we knew. My idea of sophistication was s'mores nachos with pretzels that Mom made on family camping trips."

He smiled, his crow's feet deepening. "That sounds nice."

As a fancy professional chef who'd run a New York restaurant that had been booked out six months in advance, Clem wouldn't have expected him to agree. Surely, they'd have to be some kind of culinary sacrilege?

She shrugged. "They were an acquired taste."

"I mean the family camping trips."

The wistfulness in Jude's voice jogged her memories. She'd forgotten until this moment how Jude's parents' unhappy relationship had dominated his childhood. How he'd looked forward to camp every summer for a chance to escape the household tension. Sure, he'd put on a brave face, acted the clown, but, because they'd been inseparable at camp, she'd seen him in all his unguarded moments, too.

And then after that fateful camp where they'd rather ridiculously *sworn each other their troth*, his parents had divorced and he'd stopped coming. They'd written—well, mostly *she'd* written—but it hadn't been the same.

YOU HAD ME AT CHOCOLATE

She sighed. "What's going on with you, Jude?"

"Nothing." He shrugged then shoved his hands in the pockets of his jeans. "I've just had a lot of time to think while I've been in Africa and I came across this pack of origami paper at JFK on my way to Khartoum, and it reminded me of your obsession with paper cranes after we took that origami lesson at camp. So, I bought it. And I searched on YouTube for videos on how to fold a paper crane."

"You didn't remember?" It had been one of the many activities they'd done together during their first ever camp.

"I remember not really being enthused during that particular activity."

His understatement surprised a laugh out of Clem. But she'd loved it and had taken to folding paper cranes all the time. She'd folded one every night before bed during that camp and all the subsequent ones and would hand it to him the next morning because it had seemed appropriate given his father's obsession with cranes and it had made him smile.

"I started to do it all the time then in my down times."

Clem was curious about his time in Africa and if they'd been meeting under much more normal circumstances, she'd have pumped him for information but nothing about tonight was normal.

"And I'd think about you whenever I was doing it. How nice and kind you always were. How you always seemed to know when I needed to talk and when I didn't want to. How you always looked out for the younger kids and how you liked to keep lists and always had goals. How organized and sensible and practical you always were. How you'd always

19

been the perfect friend."

Organized. Sensible. Practical.

Sweet baby Jesus. Clem almost rolled her eyes at the insipid compliments. What woman ever tired of hearing man talk about her like that?

But his eyes—green, pale as peridots—were sincere and imploring, clearly wanting her to understand so she nodded and said, "Thank you," with as little stiffness as possible.

"I also thought about how fast I'd been living. How I was trying to be everything to everyone. Trying to prove that I could make it. Prioritizing *stuff* over people. Needing all the newest gadgets from a stick blender that could practically read your mind to the latest sports car. Being seen at all the right places all while striving to stay one step ahead of the restaurant competition, which is *cutthroat*, let me tell you. Burning the candle at both ends."

"Sounds exhausting."

"It was. I was running on empty. I just didn't realize it until everything imploded."

"Yes. I saw the video."

The footage, taken by a diner at the restaurant, had gone viral. Jude had been caught on camera ranting at a customer who had been rude to one of the waitstaff—that part *hadn't*, however, made it onto the video! The guy had clearly deserved to be put in his place but when he'd told Jude to mind his own business it had escalated. Jude, his patience clearly hanging on by a thread, had given him a shove in the chest when he'd stood and loomed threateningly. Then the customer had taken a swing so Jude had returned fire.

Except the customer turned out to be some minor Euro-

YOU HAD ME AT CHOCOLATE

pean royalty. With bodyguards.

A melee ensued during which the police got involved and Jude was arrested. The charges were dropped the next day but then a few days later, a wannabe Instagram influencer seeing a shot at her fifteen minutes of fame, posted a video of her and two friends doing lines of coke in the restaurant restroom. Because of the previous incident the post had also gone viral.

Within a week, he'd sold *Hey Jude* to a friend of his who owned two other Manhattan restaurants and he'd dropped out. Disappeared. To Africa.

"When my year was suddenly up last week, I started to worry about going back to the rat race, getting back on that treadmill. I didn't want to, but I didn't know what else to do either. Except I had all these paper cranes and this gut urge to see you and our birthdays were looming and I remembered our pact and everything just fell into place."

Clem frowned. What the hell did that mean? "What do you mean, everything fell in place?"

He walked forward and Clem didn't stop him as he covered the distance between them. Reaching out his hands, he took hers, holding them between their bodies like they were already standing at the end of a flower strewn aisle, the origami crane squashed in her left hand.

"You're who I need in my life. What I need. To start anew. I can't go back to what I had—I don't want to. I need to surround myself with people who represent what I want going forward. Not fast lane, not celebrity. The quiet life. I've been thinking about that little inn in the countryside I always wanted but which somehow got lost in flashier goals

21

AMY ANDREWS

along the way. And I need a woman by my side who is dedicated and diligent and goal driven. Who's hard working and focused, who can help me with my dreams."

A tiny spot of cold made itself known in the center of Clem's stomach. Like an ice cube shoved into her belly button. It spread freezing tentacles down to her toes and out to her fingertips and burrowing deep into her chest, chilling everything in its path.

It seemed like Jude's ego had learned squat from his self-imposed ostracism in Africa. *I* need. *I* need. *I* need.

Help *me*. Help *me*.

"I need a woman who can help me be a better man, Clementine."

Chapter Two

CLEM COULDN'T BELIEVE that her brain could be at boiling point when her body was suffering from a cold flash of arctic proportions. But cold was better, she figured. Frostiness was the right way to get through this when she had a hundred plus people partying just outside her door. For damn sure he deserved a roasting but the ice in her veins would help her to keep things in check. Help her be logical rather than emotional.

Instead of flame thrower, he'd get polar plunge.

"Wow," she said, her voice dripping with sarcasm and icicles as she withdrew her hands. "You sure know how to sweep a woman off her feet."

He winced and she almost felt sorry for him.

"I'm sorry…" He raked a hand through his hair. "I'm screwing this up."

Oh, you have no idea, buddy.

"No, no, do go on," she dismissed on a wintery blast of civility as she moved over to her window which looked over the street. Placing the paper crane down on one of two piles of books sitting on the deep sill, she crossed her arms as she turned to face him. "How do you figure this will go down? We just pick the next available date at the church and I get a dress and we do the deed?"

He shuffled his feet, shoved his hands in his pockets. "No, of course not. I guess we'll ... spend the next few months getting to know each other again, renew our friendship first. Go from there."

Clem had to bite the inside of her cheek to stop from pulling a face. Or screaming. Getting married might not be on her radar for the foreseeable future, but she had thought about it at various stages of her life. Thought about who the guy might be and how that life might look. And it was nothing like this horribly bland proposition Jude was offering.

She wanted *spark*. She wanted fireworks and giddiness and that crazy leap in the pulse. And, and, and... Her brain whispered, *tummy wobbles*, and she quashed it ruthlessly.

"Yeah." She shook her head. "That's not going to suit me, I'm afraid."

If he was taken back by her rebuttal he didn't show it, he just sent her a lopsided smile. "What," he said, his voice light, "you don't want to think it over a little first?"

Man... she didn't know how big his balls had been at twelve but she sure knew the size of them now. He clearly had giant cahones.

"You know, I can't decide if this is celebrity arrogance or male ignorance."

He spread his hands in appeal. "I'm just saying, why not sleep on it?"

She sent him a thin smile. "Nope. Leaving aside the utter ballsiness of your assumptions, I am *leaving* in two days for an *eight-week* Mediterranean tour. And if you think for a single solitary second, I'll be mulling over this ridiculous proposal then you're wrong because when I get home, I'm selling up and moving to New York. I have a job starting there in January."

"You're..." He stared at her, a confused *V* forming between his eyebrows. "Leaving?"

"Uh, *yeah*." She bugged her eyes at him. "And maybe if you'd called ahead, got in touch somehow, I could have saved you the trip."

Clem watched as the information sank into his brain, watched a range of expressions chase each other across his face, his brain obviously ticking away.

"You're... moving to New York?"

"Yeah. Ironic, right?"

The fact he was fleeing the Big Apple just as she was about to take her first big bite out of it didn't really fit in with his whole pinkie swear destiny narrative. She sighed, suddenly not mad, just exasperated that he would think she would drop everything to be with him and prioritize *his* life, *his* hopes, *his* dreams.

She was at a crossroads here, too. But she was forging her own way.

"This is not just my birthday party, it's my leaving party. My last day at the library is tomorrow. So I'm not going to marry you, Jude. And you shouldn't marry anyone else either—not in your current state of mind. What you *need* is to not be with anyone. You need to figure this out for yourself. I, or any other woman for that matter, wasn't put on this earth to help you do *squat*."

Too many people had clearly *yes, chef*ed him for too long.

25

"Certainly not to make you a better man," she continued, on a roll. "The Jude I knew already was a good person—go find him. And then go find an inn and make *your* dream come true. I know you're used to having an entourage at your disposal, a lot of yes people around you telling you how fabulous you are but I'm not one of them."

He gave a humorless half laugh. "No, please, tell me how you really feel."

Clem refused to feel sorry for him or to back down. He was a grown adult who had, by any measure, made an outstanding success of his life. So... he was going through some stuff. Who wasn't? He'd figure it out. Without marrying her—marrying *anyone* she hoped—in the process. "This is *your* dream, Jude. *You* make it happen."

"I have built up a restaurant from scratch, you know. I'm not a novice."

It was her turn to laugh. "No, you didn't." Was he for real? "You'd become a mega television star on the world's most watched cooking show. You can't tell me that all the right people weren't laying out the red carpet for you. Tying themselves in knots to help you. Taking any little hiccup or problem and solving it for you."

She didn't know that for sure, but she followed his career enough to know that he suddenly had a lot of rich backers including a major television network who'd filmed a documentary on the process. To launch a new restaurant in New York within months of his win had been no mean feat but his celebrity had helped. As had hosting a bunch of Hollywood A-listers every night of the week.

"Truly starting from scratch is a lot scarier than that. But

YOU HAD ME AT CHOCOLATE

if it's your dream and you're committed enough then you can achieve it. And it'll be so much more satisfying because you did it by yourself. Like you did when you took yourself off to France all those years ago."

Jude had left home three days after his high school graduation, putting his ass on a plane for Charles de Gaulle determined to be a chef. He'd posted her a letter on his way to the airport—the last one he'd ever sent her.

"*That's* what you need now—personal accomplishment. No leg ups. No helping hands. And if a woman comes along in the midst of all that because suddenly you're happier and more fulfilled than you've ever been in your life and you fall head over heels in love…"

Clem faltered. The idea of him falling in love with someone caused a tiny squall in her belly. Which she ignored. She hadn't seen Jude Barlow in years and rarely thought about him. She had zero time for belly squalls.

Or wobbles.

"Then that's the cherry on the top." Absently, Clem realized she'd used a culinary reference. "That's the way it *should* be." Not from some stupid marriage pact they'd had no business in making. At *twelve*. Like they'd been the kid actors in some Hollywood rom-com.

"You always did have your act together," Jude said with a wry kind of smile.

Clem wasn't so sure she was a great example given how mundane her life had become when she hadn't been looking. But she was going after what she wanted *now*. And so should he. "Just… go home, Jude."

He looked at her for long moments through those pale,

27

bleary eyes then rubbed a hand over his face in the way of the truly exhausted. His whiskers scraped against his palm as he absently ran his fingers along his jaw and Clem felt the delicious frisson of it in the sudden hardening of her nipples.

Clearly, she was *not* exhausted.

"I don't even know where home is anymore."

His mother had mentioned that he'd sold his apartment in New York so Clem figured that wasn't a possibility but it wasn't like Jude freaking Barlow didn't have options. "Why not go see your mom?"

"I will soon but…" He nodded his head slowly as if he was deciding something on the spot. "I think I'm going to hang around Marietta for a while."

A crazy little pulse leap caused a spike in Clem's temper. The rub of her erect nipples against her bra only added to her ire. "If you think I'm going to change my mind when I get back then let me disabuse you of that right now."

"I know, I know. I get it. I just…" He shrugged. "I need to sleep for a week and then I've got a lot of thinking to do."

"Wasn't that what Africa was about?"

"Africa was about…" He gave a half laugh. "Shedding my ego. Letting go of the last ten years. Not thinking about the next ten. I only really thought about what was next in that last week and when I got on that plane and didn't know my next move, I guess I just panicked. Combine that with jet lag and…"

Clem nodded. "You wound up in Marietta."

"Right." He grimaced. "And now I have to change course. Rejig. And that'll be easier to do that away from distractions. So… why not here?"

Clem shot him an incredulous look. "Really?"

"Sure. Why not?"

"Because it's not Paris. It's not New York. You can't walk down the main street at midnight and get a slice of pizza or see a show."

He shrugged and, *god help her*, Clem's gaze drifted to how well those shoulders filled out his sleeves. "Couldn't do that in the Sudan, either."

Glaring at him she said, "You know what I mean."

"Who knows? I might even find an inn around here."

And then, as if to emphasize the point that he wasn't going anywhere, he stuffed his hands in the front pockets of his jeans pulling the low riders down a little, exposing flat, lower abs lovingly hugged in khaki.

Annoyed that she'd noticed, Clem dragged her gaze back to his face and her head back into the conversation. "You're serious?"

He shrugged. "It's scenic, there's mountains nearby. Seems like it might be the perfect spot for a country inn."

"It sounds like you're half-assing this."

"It'll sound better after I've slept for the next thirty-six hours."

Clem bit back on the urge to ask him where he was staying. Hospitality had been ingrained in her and ordinarily she'd have offered him her spare room but given his very public marriage proposal she didn't need that kind of speculation.

Or her mother picking out china patterns.

"You know *nothing* about Marietta."

"You're wrong. You always spoke so glowingly of it, I feel

like I already know it. And besides…" he said, his voice teasing, "an old friend lives here. I'd like to stay and get reacquainted with her."

Clem's belly performed a slow loop-the-loop and she absently flattened her hand against her stomach. Was it her imagination or had that tease in his voice made *reacquainted* sound a little dirty?

As if he knew it, he clarified. "As friends." He pulled a hand out of his pocket and drew a cross over the center of his chest. "Come on, Clementine, please."

"You don't need my permission to stay," she muttered waspishly. She sincerely doubted he was still going to be here in two months, anyway.

"No, but I'd like to have your blessing."

"Fine." She huffed out a breath. She could hardly stop the man from staying in her hometown. "Friends."

He grinned. "Good."

"I mean it, Jude, *friends*," she reiterated because his grinning was doing even worse things to her belly than his voice. "I'm going to the Mediterranean in two days and I'm going to flirt with a lot of men."

"Okay."

Clem didn't know why, but Jude's apparent unconcern about the flirting needled almost as much as his completely practical, utterly passionless proposal. "I'm probably going to kiss them, too," she goaded. "Italian men. Greek men. Spanish men."

"They'll be lining up, I'm sure."

His lack of interest in her kissing every guy in the entire Mediterranean bothered her—a lot. "I'm not *twelve* any-

YOU HAD ME AT CHOCOLATE

more."

"Yes." He smiled, big and slow, his eyes giving her body a much more thorough once-over, lingering on her mouth and her breasts and her thighs, blasting heat through her system. "I can see that."

The muffled sound of a glass smashing against what sounded like her kitchen tiles—the third tonight—jerked Clem away from the sticky pull of his gaze.

She straightened. "You need to leave now." She didn't care how rude it sounded but the last thing she wanted was Jude freaking Barlow hanging around the party causing all kinds of speculation.

He nodded apparently unconcerned at her directive. "My bed at the Graff awaits."

Of course, he was staying at the fanciest hotel in town. "If you're still here when I get back—"

"I will be," he interrupted swiftly and definitively.

"Well… in that case I'll see you then."

"I'm already counting down the days," he said as he slowly backed away. "Don't forget to make a wish when you cut your cake." Then he turned, all broad back, narrow hips and long, loose stride as he crossed the room and let himself out.

Clem shut her eyes against the tempting pull of two very fine glutes and wished she'd never ever pinkie sworn on *anything* with Jude Barlow.

❧

JUDE WOKE AT three the next afternoon. It wasn't thirty-six

31

hours but it was substantial. He was thirsty, starving, and dying for a piss. But none of those things trumped the memory of his ridiculously foolhardy marriage proposal at Clementine's party last night.

He picked up one of the plump, snowy-white pillows discarded on the bed beside him and covered his face letting out a long groan at his utter stupidity. What had he been thinking? Asking *any* woman to marry him in his zombie-like state, let alone one he'd last seen when he was *twelve*?

When she hadn't even been a woman.

At her birthday party—her *leaving* party. In front of all of her friends. *Way to put her on the spot, douchebag.*

He wished he could have blamed being drunk or a recent blow to the head but it appeared extreme jet lag had resulted in him taking temporary leave of his senses. Unless it was some kind of weird African water-borne amoebic illness that was eating away at his brain? That could explain it. In fact, it would be preferable right now to be able to blame a deadly disease rather than himself for his faux pas.

Jude yanked the pillow off his head as his brain snagged on the other salient point from last night. *Clementine was leaving.* First to the Mediterranean then to New York. He'd arrived and she was on her way out. The well of disappointment inside him stretched deep and wide and that would be something to ponder in the weeks ahead but right now he circled back to the terrible assumptions he'd made that had led him to her door.

He hadn't even stopped to consider these past few days that she might have plans. Plans that *didn't* include him.

"Fuck," he muttered to the empty room.

YOU HAD ME AT CHOCOLATE

He had to go and apologize. If it wasn't too late. Sure, he'd been contrite last night but that needed to also come from the cold light of day.

Dragging himself out of bed he stepped over the clothes he'd shed last night before crashing face down on the mattress and hobbled to the bathroom where he emptied his bladder, drank three glasses of water, then threw himself in the shower.

A cold one.

By the time he stepped out, his skin was buzzing and he actually felt alive again. Foolish, still, but definitely like a fully functioning member of the human race. A responsible adult. Instead of an impulsive, egotistical asshole tripping all over his own damn ego.

Throwing on some fresh jeans, a button-down shirt and a pair of boots, Jude left the room in search of Clementine. According to what she'd told him, she had one day left at work so hopefully she'd still be there. He'd call there, first, anyway then try her house.

Or, the scene of the crime as he was coming to think of it...

It was a pleasant day in Marietta as he navigated to Main Street, cold but clear, the sky an endless kind of blue. He'd arrived in town after eight last night and had paid little heed to his surroundings as he'd walked to Clementine's but the leaves were changing on the dogwoods he noticed.

Autumn was hitting its stride.

Turning right, his legs ate up the distance to the library. Jude couldn't help but be charmed by the old-world feel to the streetscape, from the carefully maintained facades of the

33

buildings to the old-fashioned lampposts lining the sidewalk. It was bustling, too, people going about their business, some stopping to chat to friends and neighbors, most nodding at him and saying hello.

He was soon standing opposite the historic sandstone courthouse at the end of Main Street. With its domed edifice and multiple formal windows it was an imposing and impressive building but paled in comparison to the majestic line of Copper Mountain rising up behind. It drew his eyes upward to the powdery dusting glistening on the very peaks. He suspected within a couple of months the giant craggy angles sawing into the sky would be covered with layers of thick snow, running down the slopes like royal icing atop a cake.

To the left of the courthouse was the library. It wasn't as grand as its neighbor but obviously also historic. Its retro red brick exterior, distinctive flat roof, lack of portico and tall windows made the whole building far less formal. More workhorse than show pony. No frills but excellent bones.

The huge central wooden door looked like it could have graced any number of barns in rural America and invited people to enter. The entire vibe was warm—inviting. Cozy. Like a library should be, he supposed. The courthouse pompously bellowed, *serious business of state is conducted here.* The library whispered, *adventures await you here.*

He could see why Clementine had wanted to be a librarian from the time they'd first met. If she got to come to work here every day he couldn't blame her. He'd felt the same way working in the Latin Quarter in Paris surrounded by hundreds of years of architectural history and the echoes of

34

millions of feet he swore he could sometimes hear whispering off the ancient cobblestone streets.

Mounting the five wide stairs he crossed the short distance to the front door, pushing on the wooden paneling. It was as heavy as it looked but it gave easily swinging open without a sound.

Jude was unprepared for what he saw on the other side of the door. What the building lacked in imposing on the outside, it made up for it on the inside, opening up as soon as he crossed the threshold into a large marble foyer dominated by a staircase leading to the floors above and a soaring ceiling. Beneath his feet, the polished red marble complemented the red bricks and was shot through with veins of milky white.

It was impressive, perhaps made even more so by the hush that pervaded the cavernous space.

Just ahead was the large wooden circulation desk and either side of that, filling the spaces was row upon row of shelves laden with books. Signs on the ends of the aisles indicated what books could be found in that section. And *QUIET PLEASE* signs were prevalent.

To his right, there was a section with what appeared to be copy machines and printers and over a dozen desks, all with a computer station. Over half of them were being used by people of varying age groups all staring earnestly at the screens, some tapping away at the keys or driving a mouse, some making notes, others engrossed in the content before them.

On the opposite side there appeared to be a children's reading section. It was partitioned off with furniture and some large bright, blocks that sported colorful posters on their inner surfaces. Several yellow and green beanbags were spread around the space and, in one corner, a two-dimensional cardboard cutout of a tree had been decorated in fall leaves made from red and orange paper and stuck haphazardly to the branches.

A kid's project, he assumed.

A quick look around the space revealed no Clementine and he crossed to the central circulation desk to inquire. Mounted on the front was a large, rectangular framed art installation, consisting of what seemed to be repurposed book pages that had been rolled back on themselves to form petals and then somehow secured together.

An African-American woman, her hair back in a tight, elegant bun, glanced up from her computer console as he approached.

"Hello there," she greeted with an open friendly smile.

Jude returned it. Maggie, according to her nametag, appeared to be in her midfifties. Her very perfunctory smile changed to *well, hello there* as she peered at him a bit harder over the top of her glasses. "How can I help you today, sir?"

He was used to being recognized by women. But this wasn't that. There wasn't that zealous light in her eyes, which always made Jude a little wary. It *was* ogling but done in a way he could only describe as… librarian. Quiet, discreet appreciation. Like he was a brand-new book complete with pristine pages, uncracked spine, and that very particular ink and paper aroma.

"I hope so." He smiled again because it was clear she knew he knew she was ogling and just didn't care. "I'm looking for Clementine Jones. I'm not sure if she's in today? She mentioned last night this was her last day?"

"Oh, yes," she said thoughtfully, sliding the glasses off her face. "You're the guy from the party? The one who proposed to her?"

It was ridiculous to be a grown man and still be capable of blushing, but it was the curse of a redhead. He'd thought he'd outgrown it but, apparently, not.

"Guilty as charged. You were there, huh?"

"Oh, yes." She grinned. "*Everyone* was there."

"Great," he said deprecatingly.

"She popped out to grab some coffees from the Java Hut. I'm surprised you didn't pass her in the street. She should be back shortly."

"Okay, thanks... I'll—" He looked around. Beyond the desks, there was an area with some comfy-looking couches, but did he want to have a conversation with Clementine in such a public place. He glanced back at Maggie who regarded him with keen interest. "I'll wait outside for her, grab her as she comes back in."

"But how on earth am I going to be able to eavesdrop on your conversation when you're all the way out there?"

Jude chuckled at her unabashed admission. "It's just an apology."

"It better be good." Maggie pushed the glasses back on her face. "She was still pretty steamed about it this morning."

Oh *crap.* "Thanks for the heads-up."

Jude departed, the door shutting silently behind him and he took the opportunity to rehearse what he was going to say as he paced back and forth along the middle step. By the time Clementine returned two minutes later, he'd practically worn a depression along the length of it. She eyed him warily as she stopped on the step beneath him, a tray of take-out cups in hand. But that wasn't what held his attention. That honor went to what she was wearing.

Her snug black T-shirt sported a stylized circular logo in the middle which was clearly the library—the red outline of a building with tall windows and a flat roof, the green triangle behind obviously Copper Mountain. She'd teamed it with a pair of what he thought could be chinos but none of the plain, muted colors he normally associated with the style. These had vertical stripes every shade of the rainbow. They looked like a bar code and the LGBTIQ flag had succumbed to a wild night of drinking and had a love child.

Teamed with purple flats she looked very… colorful.

"Well… that is not what I pictured you wearing to work." It was certainly different to Maggie's demure blouse.

She rolled her eyes. "Let me guess… tight skirt, kitten heels, twinset, glasses, and hair in a bun that I can just pull out and have it all cascade down my back with one shake of my head."

Jude started guiltily. He'd never thought of Clementine in that kind of way but, for some reason, the image of *librarian* in his head was straight out of porn central.

Deciding to let him off the hook she asked, "Why are you here, Jude?"

"Don't worry, it's not to propose again."

She didn't crack a smile as she climbed to his step then moved up another which put them at eye level. "I should hope not."

It took a beat for him to answer, momentarily distracted by the bounce in her springy curls. "It's an apology."

"Accepted."

Jude blinked. The last woman he'd dated for any length of time had sulked for days after they'd disagreed. "You haven't heard it yet."

She lifted the tray of drinks. "The coffee's getting cold."

Right, so, *spit it out*, man. Jude cleared his throat. "I realize I must have sounded like an egotistical dick last night. It was your birthday and I made it all about me. I apologize for embarrassing you in front of your friends."

"I think you probably embarrassed yourself more."

Jude chuckled. Clementine had always been blunt. "It's no excuse but I think I underestimated how badly jet-lagged I was."

Her eyebrows rose. "You think?"

"I really am sorry. It just seemed kinda *right* after feeling adrift on top of traveling for four days through about a dozen different time zones. I acted impulsively."

"Look, I've been jet-lagged myself so I understand how it can screw with you, but clearly you and international date lines are not a good mix. You should keep in mind that next time you propose to a woman under the influence of jet lag, she might just say yes."

Jude snorted. "Next time I will chain myself to my bed for a week and employ around-the-clock security."

She smiled, emphasising those chipmunk cheeks. "Good plan."

Then they were both smiling at each other. On the steps of the library. Like they were the only two people in the world. It felt good—familiar—like it always had with Clementine despite how long it had been. But something about it also felt new. Felt different.

Her smiled dimmed a little as if she could feel it too. "Okay… well, if that's all, I gotta—" She raised the tray of take-out coffees. "Deliver these."

"Oh, sorry, yes, of course." Jude backed down a step.

He went to thank her again for being so understanding and tell her how much he admired her for having drive and purpose in her life—no matter how much it'd messed with his hairbrained plans. But, before he could, a woman, powering up the stairs hunched into a jacket, her head down, almost barged right through the middle of them. She corrected herself at the last moment lifting her head to apologize.

"Oh god, I'm so sorry."

Her eyes were red, her sooty lashes damp, her voice thick with emotion.

"Tamsin?" Clementine grabbed the young woman by the upper arm with her spare hand. "Goodness, what's the matter?"

"Oh, Clem," she wailed and then dissolved into tears.

Jude cocked an eyebrow as he took the tray off Clementine so she could offer proper comfort. She shook her head at him clearly puzzled by the outburst as her arms went around the woman's shoulders and she said, "Hey there, you're okay now."

"It's not, everything is r-ru-ruined," Tamsin sobbed.

"Oh, I'm sure it's not that bad," she soothed.

"It is. The bakery in Bozeman doing the cake has just

YOU HAD ME AT CHOCOLATE

burned down which is t-t-terrible but they obviously can't do the cake and the wedding is in two *daaaaays*."

"She's getting married?" Jude mouthed over the sobbing woman's head.

"Saturday," Clementine confirmed, also mouthing.

"Every baker that does wedding cakes in the whole of Montana has been booked out for months."

Jude felt ill for the baker—having your business destroyed like that must be devastating. But he felt terrible for Tamsin, too.

"Hush," Clementine crooned. "We'll figure something out. Hell, if all else fails, the whole town can band together and make you a mountain of cupcakes."

Unfortunately, that only made Tamsin cry harder.

Before he knew it and definitely before he could stop himself, Jude said, "I can do you a cake."

Clementine flashed him a startled look. "You can?"

The young woman stopped crying and lifted her head off Clementine's shoulder—wiping at her eyes and nose. She regarded him doubtfully.

"Sure," he confirmed. "I'll need a kitchen."

"You could use mine?"

"I'll need a professional one for space and product and hygiene reasons. Do you know who the head chef is at the Graff?"

"Edwin Vidal."

"Do you think he might be okay if I used the kitchen there?"

"I… don't see why not? You're well credentialed."

"Okay." Jude nodded. "I'll talk to him."

41

AMY ANDREWS

Tamsin stared at him blankly for a beat or two before she glanced at Clementine as if seeking clarification.

"Sorry," Clementine said. "Allow me to introduce you to celebrity chef, Jude Barlow. It was probably a bit before your time but he won the first ever *Yes, Chef* and had his own fancy New York restaurant for many years."

"Oh," she said, sniffling as she eyed him speculatively. "You're the guy who proposed to Clem last night? You're hashtag rude Jude." She slid a hand over her mouth, her cheeks pinking up. "God… sorry. *That* was rude."

Jude shook his head dismissively. It wasn't the first time he'd heard it, wouldn't be the last but it had been a while. Just over a year since the hashtag had exploded on social media and, clearly, he hadn't yet lived it down. "That's me," he said pleasantly, trying to put the younger woman at ease despite not missing the notoriety of that hashtag. He held out his hand. "Pleased to meet you, Tamsin."

"Tamsin is Maggie's daughter," Clementine explained. "Maggie and I have been working together for the past eight years."

"Oh, yes." Jude smiled at Tamsin as they shook hands. "I met your mother inside earlier."

Tamsin regarded him hesitantly. "Could you make a wedding cake in two days? There's a lot of people coming and it's quite fancy."

"I cut my teeth on fancy cakes."

Jude had apprenticed at a top culinary school in Paris and he'd paid his way through by working at a small but popular patisserie owned and run by an eccentric octogenarian French woman called Madam Fontaine who had been

YOU HAD ME AT CHOCOLATE

regarded as one of the city's finest chocolatiers in her day. She'd been a hard taskmaster but had taken him under her wing and Jude had not squandered that opportunity.

He doubted Tamsin's wedding cake would be as challenging as some of the stuff Madam Fontaine had insisted he learn.

"But…" She shook her head, tears welling again. "I can't afford to get another cake. We'll get our money back eventually but I've already blown the budget so much I'm sure Daddy's rocking in a corner somewhere."

"No charge," he said quickly. "Consider it a wedding gift."

If he was serious about staying in Marietta—and in the cold light of day he realized he was—then he wanted the community to embrace him. To like him. To not think of him as some kind of brash, *rude* celebrity city chef. *As a hashtag.* Who'd appeared out of the blue and proceeded to screw up big-time by asking hometown girl Clementine Jones to marry him at her leaving party.

He'd also appreciate their support in recommending the inn to outsiders and tourists alike when it got up and running so there was no harm in some good PR, right?

Tamsin was looking at him with a mix of hopefulness and doubt and he smiled at her reassuringly. "Do you have a picture of your cake?" He knew from a decade in the restaurant business that most brides these days had Pinterest boards full of images that covered every *minute* detail of their wedding.

"Yes."

"How about this then? You give me half an hour to talk

to the chef at the Graff and then come to the lobby and we'll discuss what you want?"

Tamsin nodded and sniffled again. "Can I bring my mom?"

"Of course, you can."

"I... thank you." She wiped at her damp eyes. "It seems so inadequate, but—"

"It will be my pleasure." Jude was about to say he was looking forward to getting back to his roots, tapping into that muscle memory but he didn't think Tamsin needed to hear that. "I promise I will make you a wedding cake that will be the envy of every bride in Montana."

Tamsin grinned for the first time, pretty and perky, practically bouncing on her toes. "Thank you, thank you," she gushed. She hugged him quickly and Jude laughed. "I gotta go tell Mom."

Clementine grinned. "Go. But take these." She grabbed the tray off Jude and thrust them at Tamsin. "Tell your mom I'll be in shortly."

Tamsin didn't need telling twice and they watched her disappear through the heavy front door of the library. "A wedding cake that will be the envy of every bride in Montana, huh?"

He dragged his attention back to Clementine. Her mouth tilted in a soft smile. "Do you doubt me?"

She regarded him for long moments. "No."

Jude grinned. It shouldn't matter whether Clementine doubted him or not but the fact that *she'd* been the one who told him he could do it when he confessed in a letter he wanted to go to culinary school in Paris, when everyone else

YOU HAD ME AT CHOCOLATE

had told him it was pipe dream, had meant a lot back then.

Her faith in him now meant even more.

"I'm just sorry I won't be here to see it."

Right. She was *leaving* tomorrow. For eight weeks. And then for good in the new year. It took every ounce of Jude's willpower not to betray his disappointment.

"I'm sure you'll see the pictures on *the 'Gram*."

She laughed and it was like the way she'd always laughed—with every bit of herself. His belly warmed at a flood of childhood memories. Scaring themselves silly with ghost stories as they roasted marshmallows around the fire at camp then laughing at how terrified they'd become.

"So…" She sobered, the amused twinkle replaced with speculation. "You're really sticking around?"

"Yeah." He nodded. "I really am." The decision sat better and better. Sure, Clementine wasn't going to be here to lean on but she'd been right—he had to do this for himself. And rebuilding his dreams, or resetting them anyway, far out of the public eye in a pretty little town appealed to him greatly. "If you've got any Realtor recommendations or know of any rentals that are going, I'd be grateful."

She grimaced. "The rental market is pretty tight here at the moment."

"Hmm. Okay… well, I'll have a look around for some longer-term accommodation while I search for a rental." It seemed decadent to live in a hotel for potentially months. He could easily afford it but it was hard to feel at home in a hotel room. "I noticed when I was booking the Graff online there's a good B and B in town."

"Yeah, Bramble House. It's usually solidly booked

though."

Her teeth dug into her bottom lip as if she was mulling something over and *different* parts of him warmed.

"Look… why don't you stay at my place while I'm overseas? The house is sitting empty and if you're sticking around then…"

Jude blinked at the very generous offer as her voice trailed off. "That would be… *great*. If you're sure?"

She flapped his hesitancy away with her hands. "I'm sure. It makes sense. My mom was going to collect the mail and water the plants for me while I was away so you can do that instead."

"It won't cause any speculation for you? Around Marietta?"

"More than you turning up out of the blue after eighteen years and asking me to marry you in front of half the town?"

He winced. "Yeah… have I mentioned how sorry I am about that?"

She sighed. "It's fine. And, yes, it might cause some gossip but it's not like I'm going to be in residence as well. And it's only until you find somewhere more permanent, which you should be able to manage in the couple of months I'm away."

"That would be such an enormous help, thank you. And I'll pay you rent."

Two arched eyebrows beetled together. "No." Clementine shook her head, her curls shifting around her head. "Absolutely not."

Jude almost laughed at the distaste in her voice. "I am good for it you know."

Her lips also betrayed her level of distaste, curling a little. "I don't charge friends rent to stay a few nights at my house."

It was heartening to know she still regarded him as a friend. She'd said so last night but he had put her on the spot. He wouldn't have blamed her for changing her mind the morning after. "It'll probably be more than a few nights."

She flicked that objection away too with another hand flap as if it was a buzzy little insect. "It's the same principle. And besides, you'd be doing me a favor. It's better security wise to have someone living in the house. We don't get much crime around here but unoccupied homes are always targets."

He smiled. "I will guard it with my life."

Nodding, she said, "Okay, I've gotta get back to work. I'm leaving first thing in the morning for New York. I'll call into the Graff on my way out and drop my housekeys at the concierge desk and you can move in tomorrow. Spare bed is at the end of the hallway."

"Cool." Jude nodded casually. She clearly didn't want him moving in while she was still there or sleeping in her bed. Which was *fine*. He was just grateful to have a home base for the next little while.

"And thanks. Again." She slipped her hand onto his forearm. "About Tamsin."

Jude's skin glowed where she touched. "Of course." He dismissed her thanks as she had dismissed his earlier.

"So, I guess… I'll see you in a couple of months."

Her hand was warm on his skin as their gazes locked. "I'll be here."

She squeezed his arm and, for a moment, she just stood

there, not moving, like she wanted to say something else but she didn't know what. "Okay. Bye then," she finally said as her hand slid away and she turned and headed for the library door, a flash of color against the dark wood panels framing her body.

"Bon voyage," he called after her.

But she didn't turn, she just let herself in, the door closing on a soft whisper of air.

Chapter Three

A T ELEVEN O'CLOCK on Saturday night, a female voice called flights over the JFK intercom as crowds of people ebbed and flowed along the concourse. But Clem was oblivious, glued as she was to Tamsin's Instagram account. The pictures that had been posted were gorgeous. Tasmin made an exquisite bride, the cream lace of her dress complementing the caramel tones of her skin, the flamenco-style ruffle at the back of the dress running all the way from her butt and widening out as it descended to form a unique train.

It was very haute couture, designed, according to Maggie, by an up-and-coming American designer.

And the way her new husband looked at her? The way they looked at each other, like they were the only two people in the room? That caused a stupid little flutter of her heart. And a stirring of the same feelings that had bubbled up a year ago—like there was more to life than the status quo.

They were clearly in love and, for a beat in time, Clem envied them. She wanted that, she realized. She wanted a man to look at her like Gary looked at Tamsin. Like she was all he ever needed. Not because she was *practical* and *sensible* but because he simply couldn't live without her. And she wanted to look at a man like Tamsin was looking at Gary.

That he was *the one* and nothing else mattered.

One day. Not now, of course. There was the Med and then New York and a whole new life waiting for her—an antidote to the status quo blues.

But some day...

Hastily pushing those feelings aside, she concentrated on the cake picture. She spread the image on her phone screen with her index finger and thumb to make it bigger so she could look at the intricate detail. And it was utterly stunning—Jude had outdone himself.

The cake would be, as he had promised, the envy of every bride in Montana.

It was four round layers, one on top of the other, the largest at the bottom. They were covered in a dark chocolate fondant-style icing from what she could tell. It was smooth and plain, no decorative touches, except for a plain coppery-brown ribbon circling the base of each layer.

But then there was the top layer. It was crowned with the most extravagant chocolate ruffle, a clear homage to Tamsin's train. It flowed down the tiers of cake like a waterfall, rippling in tight waves that almost looked like flowers, widening as it descended, mimicking the dress, into a river of chocolate fondant as glorious and alive as the swish of a flamenco dancers skirt.

It was so rich, so intricate. It must have taken him *hours* of work.

Opening her texts, she navigated to the conversation between her and Jude. She'd left her cell number with the keys at the concierge desk in case he needed to contact her with

YOU HAD ME AT CHOCOLATE

some kind of house emergency. But he'd texted her last night to thank her again and let her know he was in and they'd been texting back and forth ever since.

He'd refused to send her picture of the cake because Tamsin had wanted the big reveal to be on Instagram but now she'd seen it, she *had* to congratulate him.

Just saw the cake!! OMG. Juuuude! Every bride in Montana is *going to want you!*

Clem wasn't sure if he'd get back to her before she boarded the plane in half an hour, which meant it would probably be another twelve hours before she got the answer because surely, he must be exhausted after his massive dose of jet lag and that magnificent cake? The immediate appearances of those three little dots had her heart skipping.

Very pleased with how it turned out. Tamsin was too.

She smiled. For a guy who had come across on TV as having an ego as big as North America, he was being surprisingly modest.

I bet she no longer doubts your abilities.

It had been disappointing to miss Tamsin's wedding but this trip had been booked first and, due to the sparsity of regional flights and the necessity for several connections to get to New York on a weekend, Clem would have missed the wedding anyway even had she left Marietta today. With over two hundred guests helping the happy couple celebrate, including her parents, Clem knew she wouldn't be missed.

Still, she would have loved to have seen that cake in real life.

She apologized for the doubting.

Clem laughed. Her phone buzzed with Jude's next text.

51

You at the airport?

Yes. Plane boards in 30.

More dots appeared on the screen. *Bon voyage. See you in December. Wish me luck on my inn hunt.*

A tiny pang of *something* caused a contraction in the center of Clem's chest. Part of her wished she could be in Marietta to help him. Not enough to forgo her Mediterranean jaunt but, damn him, why hadn't he contacted her first? She could have been useful. Not as his *wife*—seriously, what had he been thinking?—but she was a librarian, research was her jam. It was what she did for a *living*. She could have done a lot of legwork for him. They could have synchronized their calendars.

He might have been an absent friend but their friendship went back a long way and she'd have been thrilled to see him move to Marietta and set up a business. She'd have been his biggest champion.

If she'd had some kind of heads-up.

Good luck! Can't wait to see what you find. Send me pics! If you need me to contact anyone about any places just let me know.

Sure, she was on vacation, so she probably shouldn't offer, but she could probably still be of some assistance to him from afar and old habits die hard. Helpfulness and responsibility were completely ingrained traits.

Deal. As long as you send me Mediterranean pics, too.

The possibilities of that request set her imagination running. How would he feel about a bikini snap? She'd packed one because the weather was milder in the Med than Montana in October. It was supposed to be a very pleasant eighty

YOU HAD ME AT CHOCOLATE

degrees in Athens when they landed so she might as well grab some sun while she could, given that it'd be freezing for months when she returned. But as they'd already established they were going to be just friends, there was no point in sending mixed messages.

She sent him a blue thumbs-up and put the phone in the side pocket of her bag. She'd call her parents soon but the woman behind the desk in an American Airlines uniform was reeling off a long list of names over the intercom in their lounge which didn't make for easy telephone conversation.

"I can't believe this time tomorrow we'll be drinking ouzo in Athens," Bella, who was siting opposite, said.

Sitting beside Clem, Merridy added, "Don't forget the baklava."

Clem had met the two women on her European Contiki trip last year. Both were from LA. It had been wonderful meeting up with them again and hanging with them this past twenty-four hours before they set out on their next adventure which they'd been planning since they'd returned from Europe.

"I've been existing on one meal a day for the past month in preparation for this," she declared. "I'm going to eat all the baklava!"

Bella and Clem laughed. Merridy's sweet tooth was legendary.

She'd *love* Jude.

Clem blinked as the thought popped into her head. And sat uncomfortably in her gut. For god's sake. She was two thousand miles from him—soon to be six thousand—why was he taking up all her brain space?

53

So… he'd proposed. That was just a weird, jet-lagged aberration. And resolved now. He needed to *get out of her head*.

"And I'm going to drink all the ouzo," Bella chimed in and they all laughed a little harder.

Clem's phone rang and her pulse kicked up a notch. It was ridiculous to think it was him. If it was, surely he'd just text like he had previously? But still, Jude had been the first place her head had gone when her cell had rung.

But it wasn't Jude. It was her father.

"Hey, Dad," Clem said, still smiling at her friends. "I was just going to ring you guys. I'm boarding in about twenty minutes."

"Oh, Clementine… thank god, you're still here."

A cold hand clutched around Clem's heart as her smile died. Her father never called her Clementine. "Dad." She sat forward in her chair, her brow furrowing. "What's wrong?"

Bella and Merridy also stopped smiling as they tuned into Clem's tone and posture.

"It's Mom."

The cold hand squeezed tighter. Her father's voice was hoarse, strained. It sounded like he was crying. Panic flared through her system, her heart beating loud in her ears. "What about Mom?"

"She… oh, Clem… she's had a stroke. It's *bad*. They've… taken her to Bozeman."

A sudden buzzing in her ears made it impossible to take anything else in. Her mom had suffered a stroke? Hot bile swished in her gut. She was only fifty-four…

Oh god. Was her mother going to *die*?

YOU HAD ME AT CHOCOLATE

Clem swallowed. "Dad?"

Her pulse was so loud in her ears, Clem had no clue if she'd whispered or yelled it but Merridy's hand slid onto Clem's shoulder and squeezed. "Clem? What's wrong?"

"Is she... do they..." She couldn't even bring herself to say the words.

"I don't know," she heard her father say but he sounded like he was underwater. "Clem... I thought she was... we'd had such a great time at the wedding, no indication... I found her on the floor about an hour after we got home... I thought she'd..."

It seemed her father couldn't bring himself to say it either. "The paramedics... they told me to pray."

Oh god.

"Okay." Clem stood. Bella and Merridy followed suit. "I'm coming home. I don't..." She couldn't think properly. She couldn't figure out her first steps. But her father didn't need to know that. "Are you in Bozeman?"

"I'm on my way now."

"Okay... I'll meet you there. I need to sort things on this end and get the first flight home but I doubt I'll be able to get there until tomorrow." Which would still be quicker than driving.

"I'm so sorry, darling. I know how much you were looking forward to your vacation."

"Oh god, Dad, it doesn't matter." Nothing mattered but her mom *not dying*.

Sure, they'd had a fractious relationship this past year with Clem not only traveling again but announcing she was moving to New York. Her mom, who hadn't been happy

55

AMY ANDREWS

since her split with Reuben, didn't understand that Clem, who had always been so settled and committed to her job and Marietta, suddenly wanted more.

But Trina Jones had only been coming from a place of love and she sure as hell didn't deserve this. "Just hang in there. And ring me as soon as you have an update, no matter the time, okay?"

"What happened?" Bella asked as Clem hung up the phone.

"My mom," she said, her hands shaking now as the information set in. "She had a stroke."

"Oh, babe." Merridy grabbed her in for a hug and Bella joined in and for a few seconds, Clem succumbed to the tsunami of emotion welling inside her and cried. But, knowing there was no time to waste she pulled out of the circle and clamped down on the tears. Shutting down the daughter side of her brain, she let the librarian take over.

"I have to get to Bozeman."

God… they were going to need to get her luggage off the flight and that would cause a massive delay for everyone but she couldn't think about that now. She had to do what needed to be done.

"Right." Bella nodded. "Let's go see the desk."

CLEM STRODE INTO Bozeman hospital at three o'clock the next afternoon. She was exhausted and sick with worry. She'd spent all her travel time on her phone researching everything she could on stroke—or CVA, cerebrovascular

56

accident, as it was known medically. The good news was how much better the outcomes for stroke were these days and there was a lot of ongoing research, which was encouraging but it was the poor outcomes that had haunted her as she'd sped across the country as fast as domestic airline scheduling allowed.

Entering the intensive care waiting room, she stifled a gasp as her gaze landed on her father. He looked terrible, the lines on his face suddenly deep crevices aging him by about twenty years more than his fifty-eight.

"Oh, Clem," he whispered as he stood, his shoulders stooped, tears running from his eyes and a terrible sense of foreboding froze her to the spot for a beat, her heart crashed in her chest.

"Is she…?"

Hal Jones shook his head. "She's still hanging in there."

His voice cracked and Clem hurried across the room, straight into his arms. She staggered a little as he leaned into her and squeezed her hard, sobbing quietly. "I can't lose her, Clemmy," he said, hoarsely. "I won't know what to do without her."

Clem held him tight, shocked to see her big, strong capable father so distressed. All her life she'd leaned on him. He'd been the quiet, solid support. Always just there, in the background, believing in her, encouraging her, giving her what she needed—physically, emotionally, financially—to be the person she wanted to be.

Not to mention loving her mom. Respecting her. Indulging her. Showing Clem through example how a man was supposed to treat a woman. How a loving relationship was supposed to be.

A girl couldn't have asked for a more perfect male role model.

Even when her mom had been upset about Clem breaking up with Reuben and booking her Contiki tour, her father had been encouraging. He'd run interference with her mom, he'd told her she had to do what she needed to do, she had to follow her dreams. He'd told her everything would be okay.

Now she knew deep in her gut, she was going to need to be *that* person for him.

Pulling away from him, she gripped his biceps firmly and locked her gaze with his. "We're not going to lose her," she said, fiercely. "Do you hear?" She shook him a little. "She's getting top-notch medical care and everyone in Marietta is praying for her."

She'd talked to her mom's doctors a half dozen times since her father's phone calls last night. They'd been very informative all along, telling Clem the blood clot had occurred in the right-side of her mother's brain which meant Trina's left side would be affected but, they'd also been very guarded in their prognosis. All they were willing to say was, should she get through these next few days in intensive care, then that was encouraging. They'd also warned Clem that, should she pull through, her mother would most probably have significant neurological deficits that would require long-term rehabilitation.

Possibly a couple of years. And that she might never get *full* function back.

Clem's research had indicated as much but it had still

YOU HAD ME AT CHOCOLATE

been sobering news when she'd desperately needed something positive. She pushed it away now, though. The most important thing was to get through these next few days.

Looking ahead was futile—this was going to be an hour-by-hour thing.

"She's going to pull through," Clem reiterated. "She is tough. She is strong." Trina had grown up on a dairy farm in Wisconsin. She'd been in the milking sheds and doing chores from the time she could walk. "Do you seriously know another woman who is tougher or stronger?"

"No," her father said, his voice tremulous as he wiped a hand across his nose.

"And you really think she's going to leave this earth before I give her a grandchild?"

He laughed. His eyes were still watery but he didn't seem so stooped anymore. "Absolutely not."

"Right then." Clem smiled and gave his arms an encouraging squeeze. "Let's go in and see her, shall we?"

<hr/>

AT SEVEN THAT night, Jude answered the knock on the door, a blast of bracing October night air hitting him in the chest. He was surprised to see the woman from Clementine's party standing there. The one in the purple skirt. Although she was in jeans and a sweater tonight.

"Hey," she said. "Sorry to interrupt your evening but Clem has asked me to come and pick up some stuff for her and take it to the hospital."

Jude frowned. *The hospital?* A spike of alarm stabbed into

59

his chest like a lance. "I'm sorry… what? What's happened? She's supposed to be in Athens."

"She didn't get to Athens. Her mom has had a stroke. Her father got to her just before she boarded the plane. She flew back to Bozeman this afternoon."

Well that explained why she hadn't answered his *how's Athens* text. He'd been disappointed then annoyed at himself for being disappointed. She was in Athens at the start of her grand adventure. And they were just friends.

He shoved a hand through his hair. "Is she… okay? Her mom?"

"They don't know yet. The stroke was significant. She's in ICU. It's touch-and-go at the moment. Clem and her dad will be staying in Bozeman for a bit. If I could just…" She gestured for him to let her in.

"Oh god, sorry…" Jude fell back and the woman entered. Clearly very familiar with the layout of the house, she headed down the corridor to Clementine's bedroom and Jude followed. "Clementine must be frantic."

"Yes, she's very worried. We all are."

God, poor Clementine. She'd been so excited about her trip and now she must feel utterly wretched.

Jude hovered on the threshold, watching as the woman crossed to the desk against the far wall. He absently noted the bookshelf to the side—one of many dotted around the house—stuffed with books, spine out. Several neat stacks sat on top. There were stacks like that everywhere, on every available surface from the kitchen to the hallway stand to the coffee table in the living room. He'd even had to remove a pile from the single-seater couch before he'd sat down to

YOU HAD ME AT CHOCOLATE

watch a movie last night.

Surprisingly—or maybe not—over half of them had been nonfiction, from biographies to history texts to scientific tomes.

He watched as Clementine's friend grabbed her laptop and its cord, shoving it in its bag. Opening the desk drawers, she hunted through until she found several different plastic folders and slid them into the side pocket of the laptop bag. Grabbing the highlighter pens from the ceramic holder next to the printer, she tossed them in as well. The colorful print just above the holder, popped against the neutral mint green of the walls.

Walking to the bedside table occupied by a leadlight lamp that could easily have been at home in a church window, she grabbed the three books sitting in that pile—they appeared to be novels—and balanced them on top of the bag. The bedspread was a kaleidoscope of pastels, falling all the way down to the floor to brush the honey-gold of the wide floorboards.

"Okay. That's it for now."

Jude frowned. "You're not taking any clothes?"

She shook her head. "Clem has two months' worth of clothes with her."

"Right." She already had a packed suitcase. He gave a deprecating smile. "I'm sorry … I don't know your name."

"It's Rhonda," she said. "Clem and I have been friends since ninth grade."

Jude smiled. "It's nice to finally *meet*"—he performed air quotes—"you, Rhonda."

She eyed him speculatively. Like she had at the night of

61

the party but, stone-cold sober, it was far more probing. Rhonda was clearly missing her vocation as a proctologist.

"You sure know how to make an entrance," she murmured. "A public marriage proposal and then a flashy wedding cake that has the whole town talking."

Grimacing, Jude took the opportunity to set the record straight. "The first was a bad case of jet lag. The second was a bad case of distressed bride." He shrugged. "I have certain skills. How could I not use them?"

Looking him up and down she returned her gaze to his face. "You're staying, then?"

"Yep."

"For Clem?"

"No," he denied, quickly. Maybe a little too quickly.

Rhonda raised an eyebrow. "Really?"

Jude swallowed as Rhonda dished out another penetrating look. "Really. I'm here for me." If Africa had been about detoxing from the treadmill of celebrity by helping those less fortunate then Marietta was about starting anew.

"Hmm." She pursed her lips as if she didn't quite believe him but didn't push any further. "Anyway... I better get these to Clem."

"Sure, okay." Jude stepped out of the doorway so Rhonda could pass. "Is there something I can do for her?" he asked as he followed her back through the house.

Rhonda looked over her shoulder at him as she reached for the doorknob. "Pray."

Jude wasn't sure prayer coming from someone with dubious connections to faith would really help the situation. "Please tell Clementine that I'm thinking of her and her mom."

Rhonda nodded as she turned the handle. "I will." Then she stepped out the door and into the cold night air.

AFTER A NIGHT of tossing and turning, Jude woke knowing exactly what he *could* do. Clementine and her father would need to eat. And he could cook. They'd need to keep their strength up if they had long days of vigil ahead of them. It would be easy, he imagined, in that situation to be so anxious that the thought of sourcing and cooking and eating food could be too overwhelming.

Easy too, he imagined, to grab something quick and not particularly nutritious. But if good, healthy, nutrient-dense food was already there…?

He remembered when his grandmother died when he'd been seven and the neighbors had showed up at the door in a steady stream, all bringing food with them. He'd asked his mother why people kept bringing food when their fridge and freezer was already overflowing. She'd said that people never knew what to do for those who were grieving but everyone had to eat.

It hadn't meant much to him at the time but it resonated with Jude now and whilst prayer wasn't his thing, cooking sure as hell was.

Armed with purpose, Jude went out as soon as the store was open and bought what he needed. Then he spent the morning in the kitchen, cooking up a storm. He had no idea what either of them were in to or if they had any allergies or

63

intolerances so he just stuck to basic food that could be spread over several meals and hoped for the best.

A huge lasagna. Chicken soup, loaded with vegetables. A mild lamb curry. He bought ripe juicy apples and oranges bursting with flavor and vegetables—broccoli, beans, corn, and carrots—that could be popped in the microwave and cooked in a few minutes and were chock-full of nutrients.

Then there was the sweet stuff. Jude was tempted to go all Parisian on them but this wasn't about showcasing his skills. It was about food that could be boxed up into individual portions, that could travel and could keep and would be perfect for a sugar hit exactly when needed. So, he baked chocolate chip cookies and fudge brownies and made bags of caramel popcorn. He also made crunchy, nutty, seedy granola to go with the sweet, creamy tubs of yogurt he'd purchased for quick, easy nutritious breakfasts.

And he made cobbler. Peach cobbler to die for because, even if only for the duration of the eating, cobbler made the world a little bit better.

Then he portioned everything into individual plastic take-out containers and loaded them in the car and was on the road for Bozeman by two in the afternoon. He still had the rental car and he needed to do something about that— maybe he'd look for something to buy after he'd dropped off at the hospital—but the most important thing was to get this food to Clementine and her father.

And, truthfully, he wanted to see her. To give her a hug and tell her, although he'd been out of her life for a long time, he was back and if she needed anything to just ask. He wanted her to know he was here for her.

YOU HAD ME AT CHOCOLATE

He wanted to be the guy she leaned on…

HALF AN HOUR later, he was striding into Bozeman hospital and riding the elevator to the ICU by quarter to three, a container of cookies in hand. When he got to the waiting room it was empty and the anticipation that had been building in his chest deflated like a popped balloon. He hadn't realized how *much* he wanted to see Clementine with his own two eyes, to know she was okay.

Until now.

Of course, she was probably in with her mom. He should have texted first to let her know he was on his way. Maybe even just found out the hotel they were staying at and dropped the food in there and left again. But he hadn't wanted to interrupt whatever she was doing and he wasn't sure about cell phone rules in the ICU.

Someone entered the room. An older man whose face was etched with worry and Jude knew without a doubt it was Clementine's father. They looked very similar. Same facial features—square jaw and chipmunk cheeks. Same nose and eyes.

"Mr. Jones?"

The other man glanced at him, his expression puzzled. "Yes?"

"Hi." He crossed the room and held out his hand. "I'm Jude. Barlow. A friend of Clementine's."

"Oh yes." The anxiety eased for a moment as he shook the proffered hand with a ghost of a smile. "You're the one

65

who proposed to her at her party."

Jude blanched. He was *never* going to live that down. "Yes, sir, I'm sorry about that—"

"No need to apologize to me," he said gruffly. "I don't understand why every young man in Marietta doesn't want to marry her. But then, I might be biased."

Jude laughed. "Yes, sir."

"It's Hal, please," he said waving away the formality with his hand. "You're staying at her place?"

"Yes. Just while she was away."

They lapsed into an awkward silence and Jude could tell Hal's mind had wandered back to the reason Clementine was home instead of kicking up her heels in the Med. "How is she doing? Your wife?"

He shook his head. "She's stable but not responsive."

The graveness of the older man's tone put an itch up Jude's spine. If Clementine was half as wretched as her father, she must be in hell right now and he knew he didn't have any right to comfort her but he hated thinking about her dealing with this on her own.

"I'm sorry to hear that."

"She's in good hands. She's a fighter." He said it like a mantra. Like he'd been saying nothing else to himself since it happened.

"I'm sure she is."

"I'm sorry." Hal shook his head as if coming out of a daze. "Clem's in with Trina. I can... go and get her if you like?"

"Oh no." Jude shook his head. He didn't want to drag Clementine away from her mother's side. "I just... well I did

YOU HAD ME AT CHOCOLATE

some cooking for the two of you. I figured it'd be one less thing to worry about." He handed over the cookies he had in his hand. "This is just for a snack, there's more in the car. I can just... take it to your hotel room if you tell me where you're staying."

"Oh... that awfully nice of you." Tears filled the other man's eyes briefly before he dropped his gaze to the plastic container. When he looked up again they were gone. Putting his hand in his pocket, he pulled out a key card. "It's the Quality Inn across the road. Room 223. Just—" He passed the key over. "Leave it at the desk on your way out."

Jude took it with a nod. "Thanks. I will."

Hal glanced over his shoulder. "I gotta get back to Trina. I'll tell Clem you stopped by."

"Thank you. Tell her to text me if she needs anything else. And I'm keeping everything crossed for a speedy recovery for your wife."

Hal patted him on the shoulder. "We all are, son. We all are."

Then he turned and shuffled away, stopping to put the cookies on the sink drainer in the small kitchenette area before he disappeared out the door.

IT WAS THURSDAY night before Clem finally made it back to Marietta but the news was good. Her mother had started to respond yesterday and she had slowly become more conscious over the course of the day. This morning when she and her father had arrived, her breathing tube had been removed and her mom's eyes had lit up at seeing them. She'd even reached for them with her good hand.

She was paralyzed down her left side, had a left-sided facial droop, and couldn't make any discernible words come out, but the way she had gripped Clem's arm with her right hand had been fierce and encouraging. There had been tears and, as the day had progressed, frustrations. They obviously had a very long way to go. But her mom was out of the immediate danger and the doctors had given them reason to hope.

By lunchtime, she'd been transferred to a ward and the tight knot of anxiety that had sat like a cold oily lump in Clem's belly had loosened a little. Her father had insisted she go home and relax for a night, sleep in her own bed, unpack her huge bag from her non-vacation and catch up with some friends. He also wanted her to collect their mail and check on things in their house.

Clem had wanted her father to take the break—he'd barely slept for the past four nights or been out of the hospital. But he'd refused. She understood that he didn't want to leave his wife of thirty-one years. It was only natural that he'd want to spend every possible moment with her, especially now she was conscious and responding.

But she was worried about her father, too.

Still, Clem had left half an hour ago feeling buoyed, daring to hope that they were through the danger period and relieved that her father was no longer looking ninety years old.

But, god… she was tired. So tired.

She hadn't slept well either this past week. Not even last

YOU HAD ME AT CHOCOLATE

night when her mother had started showing signs of improvement during the day. The nurses had warned them not to get their hopes up, that it could be only temporary and that recovery from stroke was long and not always linear. Clem had lain awake half the night after a couple of hours of research into clinical trials available for stroke patients, imagining how awful it would be to return in the morning and find her mom had relapsed.

But she hadn't. She'd kept improving, and now she was in a ward, and Clem would be lying if she admitted to not being glad for a night at home in her own bed. The hotel they'd checked into had been chosen for proximity alone but it was also budget. Which meant the beds were budget.

Nothing like her dream-topper mattress that cradled her like a cloud.

The warm hug of central heating and the aroma of roasting meat greeted her as she opened her front door, dragging her heavy bag inside with her. She'd texted Jude a couple of hours ago to let him know she'd be home for the night. He'd offered to get a room at the Graff but she'd insisted he stay. With her mouth now watering, she was damned pleased she had.

A sudden burn of tears heated the backs of Clem's eyes and she blinked them back. Sitting by her mother's bedside in ICU, surrounded by tubes, and watching a machine breathe for her had been utterly terrifying and, consequently, she was in a heightened emotional state. But holy crap, she was going to need to pull herself together or she'd do something mortifying.

Like cry all over Jude.

AMY ANDREWS

She'd managed to keep her shit together these past few days and she refused to lose it now—not when things were looking up.

"Oh, hey." Jude came out from the kitchen, spying her still in the entranceway. He leaned his shoulder into the doorframe, folding his arms across his chest, meaty biceps stretching his Henley. "You're home."

Oh god. Clem blinked back a fresh wave of hot tears. *Don't* cry. Do *not* cry in front of Jude. *Pull yourself together, woman!* It didn't matter that her mom had had a stroke, that her dad had aged overnight, or that she was *tired*. The crick in her neck from the awful bed, didn't matter, either. None of those were Jude's problem and just because he was in her house all big and broad and warm looking like he belonged in her kitchen, didn't give her permission to unload.

But, *ugh*, he was a sight for sore, red eyes with his jeans slung low on his hips, a tea towel hanging from a belt loop and his feet bare. He didn't look like a TV chef or even her old friend. He looked like a... gift from the universe. A big, brawny, *sexy* gift sent to feed her during the worst week of her life. The meals he had left at the hotel had been a godsend, considering she'd been existing on chips and candy bars from the vending machine. And whatever in hell he was cooking right now, her stomach growled in appreciation.

"Yes."

They didn't say anything for long moments. Maybe he was waiting for her to add some more? But Clem was barely holding herself together right now.

"Are you okay?"

The soft inquiry had Clem biting her lip hard as she

YOU HAD ME AT CHOCOLATE

blinked back another wash of tears. *God.* She was so *not* okay but this was utterly ridiculous. For Pete's sake—she'd seen Rhonda every day this week and hadn't burst into tears upon seeing her once. Her nostrils flared as she desperately sucked in air through her nose to stop herself from cracking.

"Clementine?"

That was what did it. *Clementine.* So gentle it sliced right through the slender thread of her emotional fortitude.

"No," she admitted her voice wobbling.

And then he was walking—striding—toward her, eating up the twenty feet between them, his figure getting more and more watery the closer he came until he was sweeping her in his arms and Clementine lost it.

She really *lost it*.

Chapter Four

THERE WERE NO dainty tears. No discreet sobs or silent, internalized, shoulder-shrug weeping. She howled—*loudly*. Her face crumpling, her hand clutching at his shirt, her lungs grabbing for air between noisy, gasping keens.

She sounded utterly feral.

Not that he seemed to mind. Nor did he try and talk her through it or tell her everything was going to be okay. He just held her, tucking her in under his chin, his big arms like bands of steel cocooning her in an oasis of calm, the solid wall of his chest providing safe harbor as everything around her pitched and tossed.

"I'm sorry," she said as she pulled away after who knew how long. "I'm okay."

There was a large damp patch on his shirt and she hoped like god it was only tears. She wiped at her nose with the back of her hand—*real* classy.

But he didn't seem to notice. He just smiled and said, "Don't be a dork. Of course you're not okay."

Clem laughed then remembering how they'd called each other dork so much as kids it had become a term of affection between them. "No. But Mom is improving. She's on the medical unit now and things are looking up. I'm just… tired

72

YOU HAD ME AT CHOCOLATE

and worried about Dad and…"

God, where did she even start?

He nodded. "Hungry."

"Well, yes, actually, that too." As if to prove the point, her stomach growled *loudly*.

"Dinner is about half an hour away. Why don't I pour you a glass of wine and you go have a nice long soak in the bath? Then get into your PJs and I'll have dinner on the table when you're done and after that you can crawl into bed and flake out for the night."

Ridiculously, her eyes watered again. "I didn't expect you to cook for me." He'd already done enough cooking.

He shrugged. "It's the only thing I *can* do."

Swallowing against the lump in her throat, Clem observed, "You sure came into my life at the right time."

"I told you, our twelve-year-old selves must have known something." He grinned. "Even if we got our wires crossed a little."

Clem wanted to slide back into his arms again but fought the urge. She wasn't crying now and given her current emotional state it wouldn't be wise to mix up her feelings. Especially when he was looking about as mouth-watering as whatever was cooking.

"Let me get you that wine. Red okay?"

She nodded. "Yes, thank you."

He turned and strode back to the kitchen. Clem stayed rooted to the spot listening to him shuffle around and then he was back again, crossing the distance and handing her a decent slug of wine in a heavy cut-crystal tumbler.

"Go have a bath," he said, his lips quirking in an amused

AMY ANDREWS

little moue as Clem stood there absently staring at him, glass in hand. "I'll take your bag to your room."

A meal, some wine, a bath, and even bellhop duties. Jude Barlow, arrogant, reality cooking-show star was a bona fide sweetheart.

"Thank you," she said, her legs finally obeying frantic signals from her brain to *shift her ass*. Because if she didn't, she might just toss her glass of wine against the wall and thank him in a way that was not appropriate for friends.

And then where would they be?

JUDE THREW ANOTHER log on the fire and prodded at the wood with a poker as the flames flared and were sucked straight up the flue. They'd retired to the living room after dinner. He'd expected her to go straight to her room—she'd looked thoroughly exhausted when she'd first arrived—but a bath and a full belly seemed to have revived her and, when he'd tried to shoo her to bed she'd said *not yet* and he'd suggested a movie together.

Perhaps he should have gone to *his* bed. Made himself scarce. Then she might not have felt obligated to sit up with him. But she'd insisted it wasn't obligation, that she just wanted to chill and *not think or talk* before hitting the sack and who was he to deny her that? Given how much she'd unburdened throughout dinner about her mother's progress and the abundance of research she'd been doing, he couldn't blame her for wanting to chill.

Although *chilling* in front of the TV had a very different

connotation these days…

Connotations that were hard to ignore when she was looking warm and cozy on the couch, her legs tucked up under her, drinking her third glass of wine and chomping on the salty caramel popcorn he'd made, her hair floating around her head in a bouncy cloud.

And then there were those PJs…

Jude had seen his fair share of women's night apparel—if only for a few moments before being discarded. He'd seen silk and satin and lace that hugged and skimmed and clung. He'd seen fancy bras and barely there thongs. He'd seen studs and snaps and rhinestones holding together wispy pieces of fabric that left nothing to the imagination.

There should be nothing remotely sexy about flannel and cotton.

But fucking hell, there was. Soft red-striped flannel pants and a snug red T-shirt that had *I WILL DEWEY DECIMATE YOU* stamped across the front. He'd laughed when he'd first seen it and then he'd realized he was staring at her chest trying to figure out if she was wearing a bra and had given himself a mental slap.

She was sad and anxious and tired. She didn't need some guy checking out her goods.

Oh, and they were *friends*.

So, they'd watched the television, her at one end of the three-seater couch, him at the other, keeping his eyes glued on the screen. The only time Jude had allowed himself to look anywhere else was when he'd stoked the fire. Clementine had, thankfully, made it easier by staying curled in her corner of the couch, content, it seemed, not to chat or draw his attention.

When he'd come to Marietta a week ago, he'd had one driving purpose—to follow through on the pinkie swear he'd made to Clementine when he'd been twelve. It had been a mistake, an idiotic impulse fueled by jet lag and desperation, with no real plan attached. Just a fistful of memories that a year away from everything had made him nostalgic for.

But meeting Clementine again had shaken something awake inside him, something that he was coming to realize, even in this short time, had always been there but he'd been too young to understand or articulate. And then too distant and self-absorbed to follow through.

Seeing her again felt *right*.

Sitting here with her felt right. And not a lot had felt right in his life for some time. So, he sure as hell didn't want to screw this up because he was inconveniently… *attracted* to his one-time best friend. Clem had become Clementine—a woman, not a girl.

The impact of which he'd stupidly not factored in to the equation.

Unfortunately, the movie eventually came to an end, as did his ability to ignore her presence. She stretched as the credits rolled and hell if his peripheral vision didn't suddenly come alive with the languorous movement.

"That was good," she said on a little sigh.

Her voice was low and sleepy and wound fingers around Jude's middle. He nodded and forced him to half turn so he was facing her. "Yes." Casually tipping his head to the side, Jude rested his temple against the couch cushion.

She sent him a goofy smile and his breath hitched. A curl

had fallen down to brush her eyelashes and a strong urge to reach out and pull on it hijacked his sensibilities. In his mind's eye, he could see himself do it, see his fingers trailing down her cheek to her jaw, see her smile slowly fade as her eyes grew all smoky and her breathing turned husky.

Thankfully, she yawned and he grabbed hold of that with both hands, flicking the TV off with the remote. "You should go to bed, you're done in."

"Yeah." Her smile widened a little. "I am. Too done in to move. Your lovely food and the wine and the fire have relaxed me to the point of paralysis."

He chuckled to cover for the image swirling in his head—him carrying her into her bedroom. "You can always sleep here. The couch is comfy and I can grab a blanket for you."

Rising, he went to grab one for her—for his sanity if nothing else—but she grabbed his hand as he passed by halting him as quickly as if she'd stuck him with a cattle prod.

"It's fine," she dismissed, tugging on his hand. "I want to sleep in my own bed. I'll go in a minute. Stay and talk to me for a bit. About you. I'm sick of talking about my stuff."

Jude forced himself to smile as he sat, closer than was desirable because she was guiding him down next to her, their hands still clasped. But, it would have been rude to remove it, right? Once he was seated she let go and he quickly withdrew from her touch but they were too close for his liking. Close enough to see the orange glow playing in her curls and across her face. Close enough to touch.

Too close for the illicit messages being whispered by his

libido.

"How are your mom and dad?" she asked.

"They're the same. You know Mom's moved into an under-sixties resort like only Florida can do and loving it. Dad is still in Orlando, working for the city and obsessed with his bird watching."

"Neither of them remarried?"

"No." Which had surprised the hell out of him. As a twelve-year-old he had mentally prepared himself for a stepparent. Or two. "My mom tells me the village where she lives is a hot bed of sex and parties though." He grimaced at the memory of that conversation.

Clementine laughed. "You don't approve?"

"I couldn't care less. Good luck to her. I'd just prefer not to hear the finer details of any liaisons."

She laughed again. "I know, right? Why do parents think it's hilarious to talk about their sex lives in front of their adult children?"

Jude laughed too, even though the last thing he wanted to be talking about—*thinking* about—was sex. "I have no idea. But they do."

Still grinning, she asked, "Do they have a good relationship now or is it still rocky?"

"It took quite a few years but they're good now. In fact, they've never been this good. They're both just… happier. Which makes their relationship happier."

"That's great. My parents are still—" She bugged her eyes. "Deliriously happy." But then her smiled slipped and she sobered as she drew her knees up to her chest and wrapped her arms around them. Her gaze met his. "I was so

78

YOU HAD ME AT CHOCOLATE

scared, Jude. Seeing Mom… like that…"

"I can only imagine," he murmured, his gaze raking her face, seeing the shadow of fear lurking in her eyes.

"I mean… she drives me batty sometimes. She hasn't been particularly supportive of me traveling or moving to New York. But she's… the captain of our team, you know? She ran her parents' dairy farm single-handed after my grandfather died when she was fifteen until Grammy sold up five years later. She's so strong and yet…"

"Hey," Jude said as her voice trailed off, pulling her back from the dark abyss of what ifs. "Her strength is a good thing. She's going to need that."

"Yeah." She nodded. "I reckon it's why she's still here."

"Reckon so, too."

"If I get to be half as strong as her I'll be happy."

Jude frowned. "What are you talking about? You're strong."

She gave a half laugh. "I'm not."

"Yes, you are. Even at eight, you were the strongest, most determined person I'd ever met. Very driven and goal orientated. And you've done everything you set out to do. You became a librarian and when you decided you wanted to see the world and stretch your wings, you did that as well."

Clementine sighed. "I haven't felt very strong this past week. I'm trying to be for Dad, but I feel like I'm always about two seconds off falling apart."

"Hey." Without thinking, Jude reached across and put a hand on her bent knee and gave it a squeeze. "You've been through a very worrying time. Even the strongest of people can buckle under extraordinary pressure."

79

"I know… I can see that in my dad. It's really taken it out of him these past few days." She shook her head. "He's looking to *me* for strength and guidance. He's leaning on *me*."

"And you'll be there for him," Jude assured. "And I'll be here for you. To lean on."

Quirking an eyebrow, she said, "You will, huh?"

"Sure." He feigned a nonchalant shrug while trying not to think about the ways she could *lean* on him. "What are friends for, right?"

"Friends…" She looked at him for long speculative moments before her gaze dropped to his hand on her knee. Jude went to withdraw it but she was already sliding hers over top trapping him there. She dropped her cheek to their interlocked fingers and closed her eyes.

After a few beats, she lifted her head, propping her chin where her cheek had been and he didn't *feel* trapped, he felt… connected.

"I wish we'd kept in contact," she murmured.

"Maybe if I'd been a more faithful correspondent we would have."

A ghost of a smile touched her lips. "You went to Paris. You were busy." Her smile turned a little sad. "We weren't kids anymore."

"It was good of you to still send a Christmas card every year. Mom used to read them out to me when she called."

"That's nice," she said, her voice low, the golden glow from the fire wrapping around them like a big warm blanket. She didn't say anything for a moment or two, just studied his features intently before a slow smile spread across her mouth.

"You got *handsome*."

Jude blinked at the unexpected compliment then he blushed and thanked god for the darkness and the heat from the fire to blame it on. "I wasn't always handsome?" he asked, tying to keep it light because he couldn't let that go to his head.

She shook her head. "You were skinny and gangly and had those ears that stuck out. But you've grown into yourself." Her eyes roamed over his face again as if to be sure of her assessment. "And your hair was the color of rust but now it's..." Lifting a hand, she furrowed her fingers into the hair at his temple, watching the action.

Jude's breath hitched at the touch, her short fingernails scraping lightly against his scalp, causing a rash of goose bumps from ear to ear that marched down his nape.

"It's darkened to this deep, chestnut which is..." Her gaze cut to him. "Very, very handsome."

This time his breath stopped somewhere between his lungs and his throat. Her gaze drifted to his mouth and his throat turned dry as a chip.

"Okay..." He gave a half-laugh. The atmosphere was loaded now with something that was way more than friendship—it *sizzled* with it. And she was tired and in an emotionally fragile state. It wasn't the time for doing what every cell in his body was urging him to do—kiss the hell out of Clementine Jones.

"I think you might have had too much to drink."

She blinked. "I've had three glasses of wine. In *three* hours. I'm not drunk. I'm not even a little bit tipsy." But she withdrew her hand from his hair. "I'm sorry," she apologized. "I've let my tongue run away from me. I didn't mean to embarrass you."

"It's fine," he dismissed, excruciatingly conscious of his hand still on her knee. "I do have big ears."

Clementine laughed. "You've grown into them very nicely though." Her gaze traveled lower, from one side of his chest to the other. "Your shoulders, too."

Jude fought to keep his ego in check at her teasing flattery. Fought to keep grounded—this wasn't flirting. It was an assessment of his changes over the years. "You turned out pretty damn nice yourself."

"Finally, a compliment." She gave an exaggerated eye roll. "I didn't think you'd noticed."

Jude sobered. "Oh... I noticed."

She waggled her eyebrows at him, her eyes twinkling. "*Really?*"

It was his turn to roll his eyes. "Yes, really."

"Like what?"

"You really *are* fishing for compliments, aren't you?"

"I think it's fair to say I've given up on fishing to cut straight to the chase."

Jude laughed. "You have."

"Do you usually make all your women work so hard for compliments?"

"*All* my women?" What the hell? And... was she counting *herself* in that number?

"Yes. *All.* There are a lot of pictures of you out there with a lot of different women."

There was no denying, Jude had enjoyed his celebrity over the years but he was no Hugh Hefner. "You've been checking me out, huh?"

"Over the years, sure. What can I say?" She shrugged. "I'm a librarian. I have ninja googling skills."

"Yeah, well, I wouldn't believe half of what you see or read on the internet." It was fair to say that about ninety percent of the stuff that had been written about him in tabloids and online was wrong.

"Hmm." She eyed him suspiciously, her lips pursed. Which was very distracting. Silence grew between them for a beat or two before she bugged her eyes at him. "*Well?*"

His brows drew together. "Well what?"

"I'm still waiting to hear a compliment? Honestly—" She shook her head. "How did you get so many women?"

Jesus, just how many women did she think he'd been with? "Would you believe through their stomachs?"

She gave a quick snort laugh. "Not for a second." And then they both laughed until it petered out and Clementine tapped her index finger on their joined hands. "Still waiting, Barlow."

"Okay, okay." He withdrew his hand with no protest from Clementine as he leaned in, pretending to inspect her face, his gaze roaming all over from the spring of curls to the fullness of her chipmunk cheeks to the tip or her nose and the pointiness of her chin. She grinned at him, clearly amused.

"Yep." He nodded solemnly. "You've grown into your teeth."

Her mouth gaped in surprise and then she hooted out a laugh. "Oh my god." She shook her head at him. "That is *not* a compliment."

"No seriously." He sat back a little as if to do a fuller assessment but mostly just to put himself out of reach of temptation. "Those two years of braces were definitely worth it."

"Well, that's good to know. I hated them."

"Yeah. I remember." Clementine had shown up at their last camp with her newly applied braces. "You couldn't stop lamenting in your letters that no boy would ever want to kiss you."

Almost as soon as it was out, Jude wished he could take the *K* word back. Jesus. *Don't talk about kissing with Clementine, dickhead.* And definitely do not *think* about kissing her, either. But it was easy in the dark with nothing but the crackle of the fire, to be lulled into reminiscing. The memories were fond and she was incredibly easy to talk to.

"That's because Billy Marsh had told me that a girl with a mouthful of metal was too off-putting to kiss. I was fourteen, it was important."

Jude remembered that letter. They'd continued to correspond on and off over the remainder of their high school years which had made not seeing her again after that last camp together a little easier.

He shook his head. "Billy Marsh was clearly an idiot."

She smiled. "I'll have you know that according to Billy Marsh, he was the stud of ninth grade."

"Color me surprised." Jude laughed. "I bet he's bald with a paunch these days and didn't do so well with the ladies outside of the gloried halls of high school."

"He's not bald. Although—" She squinted as if trying to recall what Billy *dufus* Marsh currently looked like. "He is thinning on top, now you come to mention it. And he did marry. Twice." Her lips twitched. "He's currently living with his mother."

It would be very bad form to crow at that morsel of information so Jude did not. Outwardly. But on the inside, he was laughing *hard*. "I rest my case."

"I remember you tried to reassure me in one of your letters that boys would still want to kiss me."

"That's because I knew how fourteen-year-old boy brains worked." Hell, he'd have cut his mouth to ribbons if a girl with braces had been up for some first-base action.

"You would have kissed a girl with braces?"

"Are you kidding? I was a gangly redhead with giant ears; I would have kissed a girl who hadn't brushed her teeth for a month."

"Eww." She laughed. "That is *gross*."

Jude grinned. "*That* is teenage boys."

Her laughter faded after a few beats and her gaze dropped to his mouth briefly and every cell in Jude's body went on high alert.

"So why didn't you ever try to kiss me?"

If Jude hadn't been aware how close they were sitting before, he was now. Now Clementine was dissecting why they hadn't made out when they'd been kids.

He shrugged. "Because we were friends. I didn't... think about you like that." He'd clearly been more of an idiot than Billy Marsh. "I didn't think you thought about me like that either? Did you..." He knew he should probably be abandoning this topic but he didn't seem to be able to stop, either. "Want me to kiss you?"

"Oh god, no."

She didn't recoil exactly but it was an emphatic rejection. Jude couldn't figure out if he was relieved or annoyed.

"I'm just wondering why we never went there. I mean… I counted down the days until I could see you again and particularly during that last camp we were at that age where kids were suddenly looking at each other differently and yet we didn't. And really—" She smiled. "We were practically engaged."

Jude chuckled. "I counted down the days to camp, too," he said. "It was such a… relief to get away from the tensions at home for those two weeks and you were part of that anticipation because you were just so easy to be around. You didn't feel the need to talk all the time like so many girls I went to school with. If you had something to say, you said it. Otherwise, you listened. You were just so *comfortable* in your skin."

He wasn't sure Clementine wanted to hear a treatise on the complexities of their childhood relationship but it was stuff Jude hadn't ever really analyzed until now.

"Maybe I didn't want to mess with that? For damn sure, I would have screwed up any kind of pass."

She smiled. "Nose bumping?"

"Definitely." He nodded. "And teeth clashing. I had zero game."

"How's your game now?"

Jude's pulse skipped a beat and he swallowed at the sudden intensity glittering in her eyes. Thanks to his celebrity, Jude had gotten pretty damn smooth pretty damn fast but… where the hell was *this* going? "I've… not had any complaints."

She raised an eyebrow. "Care to prove it?"

A hot surge of what could only be described as lust flooded Jude's veins. Hot and rich and demanding, wrapping sticky fingers around his gut, shooting flaming arrows directly at his groin. And if another woman had asked him that question, he'd have proven the fuck out of it, but this was *Clementine* and he found himself trapped between the thrum of desire and an abundance of caution.

Christ, why had he even opened the door to a kissing conversation? *Dufus.*

"You *are* drunk," he said with a husky laugh, desperate to lighten the moment.

Slowly shaking her head, Clementine said, "Nope." Then she drew an X over the left side of her chest. "Cross my heart."

Dragging his eyes off her *boob*, Jude drew in a ragged breath, his brain scrambling between what he felt was the *right* thing to do in this suddenly weird moment and what he *really* wanted to do.

"I take it from your silence you don't..." Her eyes drifted to his mouth and lingered for a bit before returning. "Want to kiss me?"

Jude's pulsed accelerated as more heat flushed to his groin. Hell no. That would be entirely the wrong way to take it. He was just... torn. Between the boundaries Clementine had already drawn up and the demands of his libido. "I... wouldn't say that."

A smile lifted one corner or her mouth. "So... you *do* want to kiss me?"

Oh, only since she'd walked through the door tonight. But he was pretty sure this boundary blurring of hers was coming from an emotional place and he didn't know where that would leave them. He sure as hell didn't want her to hate herself—or him—in the morning.

The tension in his quads and in his inner thighs as he held himself as distant as he could, cranked a little tighter. Still… he couldn't help but ask. "Do *you* want to kiss *me*?"

"Yeah." She nodded slowly. "I really think I do."

Well, *fuck*… that was knowledge he could have done without as tension crept from his thighs to his balls. Shutting his eyes briefly, he gathered his wits. Opening them again, Jude locked his gaze on hers. "Okay…" He cleared his throat. "What's going on, Clementine?"

"I—"

Her shoulders straightened and her lips pressed into a line and, for a second, Jude thought she was going to tough it out but, in the next second, she practically deflated before his eyes. Gaze dropping to her lap, she flopped back into the corner of the couch.

"Oh, *god*. Forget it." She glanced up. There was color in her cheeks and her amber eyes could barely meet his. "I'm so sorry, it was a stupid idea." She waved her hand as if she was swatting it away. "And completely *unforgivable* of me to ask. Talk about mixed signals. *Ugh*." She sat forward, sliding her hand onto his arm, clamping on tight. "Please don't hate me."

Jude gave a wry smile at her earnestness. "I could never hate you. Just talk to me. Help me understand what's going on."

YOU HAD ME AT CHOCOLATE

She barked out a laugh. "If only I knew. I'm sorry, I just… I need… I needed…" She scowled as she looked down at where she was clutching his arm. "Oh god," she wailed. "I'm a *horrible* person."

Smiling, he gently lifted her chin. He didn't want to see her like this—mortified, wretched, wrestling with all this emotion when she'd already had to deal with so much this week. "What do you need, Clementine? You can tell me."

Her chin might have been in his grasp but she resisted looking at him, fixing her gaze somewhere near his ear instead. "It doesn't matter."

"Maybe it'll help, talking about it?"

She snorted. "Trust me, it made more sense inside my head."

Jude chuckled. "A lot of things do." With her still looking at his ear, Jude didn't hold out much hope that she was going to reveal anything. Maybe he should broach the subject? "Why did you want me to kiss you, Clementine? Were you looking to…" He hesitated not wanting to get her motivations wrong but, considering she'd been so adamant about the state of their relationship, her reversal was stark. "Take this to a friend's with benefits situation?"

Her gaze snapped to his, her eyes wide. "*No.*" She shook her head emphatically, displacing his fingers as her curls bounced around her face.

Okay, so that was a no then…

"I just… needed tonight… A distraction for *one* night from all the things that chase each other around and around in my head when I go to bed."

Her admission stopped his breath in his lungs. *Jesus.* She

89

wanted a… one-night stand? Not just making out on the couch like horny teenagers.

Going all the way.

"But that was wrong of me," she continued, "and I'm so, *so*, sorry. Using you like that, to… forget, is awful."

Jude pulled himself back from thoughts of hitting a homerun with Clementine Jones to concentrate on what she'd said. *Concentrate*, damn it. Forcing a nonchalant shrug, he said, "I've been used for worse."

He'd had women sleep with him to meet other celebrities, to make money selling a nonconsensual dick pic to a tabloid and to bump up their Instagram followers. Clementine's reasons were pure by comparison.

"Oh god, really?" She blinked at him. "That sounds terrible. I'm… so sorry."

"It's fine," he dismissed, touched by her soft apology. "Nobody put a gun to my head."

Truth was, he hadn't regretted too many of his liaisons even though accumulatively, he'd grown tired of the game. It had all seemed so empty, especially now, with Clementine sitting so close, mortified by her proposition which had been the antithesis of so many others he'd had in the past.

He'd certainly had more sophisticated seductions. But none as sweet. None he'd wanted more.

"So…" Jude's gaze fanned over her face, his heart thumping a little louder in his chest at the prospect. "One night, huh?"

A small smile lifted the corners of her mouth. "I suppose I've shocked you."

Jude returned her smile. "A little."

YOU HAD ME AT CHOCOLATE

"Because I'm a small-town librarian and therefore must be some kind of virginal prude who swoons the second a penis comes out? Or because we're friends and there are probably a million reasons why doing this is dumb?"

"Definitely the latter." There were, no doubt, many reasons why a night together wasn't wise but the fact that Clementine was after a little oblivion and she'd asked *him* was enough for now.

They'd figure the rest out later.

"Do people really think librarians are virginal prudes?"

"Some do. But for the record, I'm not a virgin and I've never fainted at the sight of a dick."

Jude laughed, tempted to say something like *that's because you haven't seen mine yet* but not succumbing. "Well, *for the record*, some people are idiots."

She grinned at him, a stray curl falling forward and, before he knew what he was doing, he was reaching for it, pulling on it, watching as it sprang back. It fell across her eye and Jude brushed it away, his fingers trailing down her cheek, to her jaw, to her mouth, her smile fading as her lips parted.

His fingers fell away, his breath roughening and falling in sync with hers as the air crackled around them like a high school chemistry set gone rogue. Jude wanted to kiss her so badly his lips tingled and his entire body trembled with the urge. He swallowed trying to remember if he'd ever felt this nervous about kissing a woman and came up empty.

Not even his first time.

But there was a *lot* riding on this kiss. If it was bad it could get very awkward around here, very quickly. If their lips met and it was an absolute fizzer—he felt nothing, she felt nothing—where did that leave them?

Somehow, though, he knew it *wouldn't* be bad.

With his heart hammering like gunshots, he leaned in, inching closer. There was probably not quite two feet separating their mouths but Jude eked out the distance, making it last as long as he could, giving her time to back the hell out if she suddenly came to her senses.

But she didn't and so there was nothing else for it than to give her what she wanted. What *he* wanted. His mouth touched down on hers, the lightest of touches before he withdrew a little to let that brief cataclysmic brushing of lips compute before he went back for more because, *fuck*, he wanted to go back for more.

"Is that it?" she whispered.

Her warm breath fanned his face, a small smile playing on her mouth.

"No," he whispered back, his hand cupping her jaw as he pressed his mouth to hers again.

And he didn't pull away this time because, holy shit, he was *kissing* Clementine Jones and her mouth was soft and sweet and she was sighing and leaning in, opening her lips to his gentle exploration, following his lead as his mouth brushed unhurriedly against hers.

His head was urging him to go faster and harder and deeper, as was the pulse washing through his ears and drumming through his chest, but he held it all in check. This wasn't that kind of situation. It wasn't a wham, bam, thank you ma'am. It wasn't some wild teenage groping in the dark. There was a lot at stake between them—their friendship—

which made it *risky*. This needed a slow hand, an easy touch.

And he had every intention of savoring it, despite the rampant state of his erection and the burn of fever in his blood.

There was citrus in her hair and cinnamon on her skin and she tasted sweet and salty like his caramel popcorn and she filled up his senses with her flavors and Jude couldn't get enough. He wanted to discover *all* her flavors.

His tongue slid out, swiping along her bottom lip, searching for traces of salt and caramel and she moaned. The kind of moan that came from a place not quite civilized. Like she'd had no control over it. And it reached right inside his underwear and squeezed. So he did it again, to her top lip, sucking on it gently this time, savoring its plumpness for long heady seconds before he dipped into her mouth, his tongue slowly exploring.

But not for long, her mouth suddenly breaking away. His muddled mind tried to identify what was wrong but then Clementine was shifting, rising up, her right leg sliding over his thighs, her knee grounding on the other side. He moved too, shifting instinctively back to accommodate her straddle, his hips and shoulders pressed against the soft fabric of the couch, his hands sliding to the backs of her pajama-clad thighs.

His head against the rest, he looked up into her face, their gazes meshing. The fire cast an orange halo around her curls which had fallen forward, contributing to the shadows darkening her face. For two people that had just indulged in the world's slowest kiss they were seriously out of breath.

"How was that?" he asked, his voice low and husky.

"Good." She smiled. "Really good."

Then, sliding her hands on either side of his face, *she* kissed *him*. It was still slow and easy, but it was deeper, her mouth opening, her tongue exploring, stroking against his until he was panting and his hands were tightening on the backs of her thighs. And when she lowered herself against him, settling into his lap, his dick reacted predictably, his hardening girth pressing against the soft fabric at the crotch of her pajamas and he groaned, his hands moving to her ass and holding tight.

She pulled away, sitting back a little, her head level with his now, her hands falling from his face. Her chest rose and fell with a gratifying unevenness. She repeated his question back at him, her voice a low, sexy vibrato. "How was that?"

He gave a ragged laugh. "Really, *really* good."

Grinning, she rose to her knees again, reaching for the hem of her shirt and hauling it over her head. There was a brief flash of pearly pink fabric and two full satin-and-lace cups before they, too, were gone and he was staring at the generous sway of her breasts.

He swallowed—hard. "You grew into your chest, too."

She laughed as she settled her ass back down. "I did."

He was conscious of her watching him, watching him stare at her breasts. And he really wished he could stop but... they were full and lush, her nipples hardening before his gaze and he wanted to *devour* them.

"Touch me," she whispered, as she plucked his right hand off her ass and brought it to her left breast. "Please touch me."

Jude's breath hissed out. Between the soft contour of her

flesh, the raw need in her voice, and the urgent throb of his body, he could no more have denied what she needed than stopped the tide from turning. He brought his other hand to her other breast and she shivered as he filled his palms with their ripeness.

When he brushed his thumbs across her nipples she whimpered. They darkened as they contracted to tight points and Jude's mouth watered at the sight. His breathing ragged, he leaned in and took one into his mouth, smelling citrus and tasting cinnamon.

She trembled against him and moaned, "*Juuuude*," shoving her hands into his hair and hell if he didn't want her even more.

Swirling his tongue around the hard tip of her nipple produced all kinds of noises from her. When he sucked and drew hard, she whimpered and when he grazed his teeth a little she gasped and bucked in his lap. He switched to the other side, keen to learn if she made different noises. It was gratifying to hear a low sort of keening when he took possession.

"Jude?" she panted, after what felt like a lot and yet *not nearly enough* time had passed.

"Mmmm?" he replied, because he could do that and still torment the hard nub he was flaying with his tongue.

But she was pulling at his hair a little and he reluctantly relinquished her nipple, lifting his head to look at her. Her cheeks were flushed and her eyes were glazed, her pupils blown and her bottom lip was sporting teeth marks.

"Take me to bed."

Chapter Five

CLEM HAD TO admire the quick and efficient way Jude followed orders. Within seconds he'd gathered her up and risen, his hands firmly on her ass. She clung to his neck, their mouths still fused as he carried her through the darkened house. And they didn't run into any walls or trip over any rugs or knock over any piles of books.

They made it to the bedroom without mishap and before she knew it, he was easing her down until her feet touched the floor.

"Condoms in the bedside table drawer," she said, wasting no time shucking off her pajama pants and stepping out of her pink underwear as she grabbed both the duvet and the top sheet in trembling hands and yanked them down.

It wasn't nerves that were giving her the shakes—it was anticipation. Hell, it was exhilaration! She probably *should* be nervous, or at least shy but, well… she wasn't. The man had already sucked on her nipples and they were about to have sex.

This was no time to be coy. Not tonight.

Tonight she wanted Jude to give her the kind of pleasure that flooded the brain, obliterating everything else. And, in the morning, they'd have to talk about how they navigated

YOU HAD ME AT CHOCOLATE

this new normal between them but, right now, he was hot and sexy and she was in full heady lust and she wouldn't be embarrassed or ashamed or *quiet* about her needs.

Clem shuffled to the middle of the bed and rolled up onto her side, elbow bent, head propped on her flattened palm watching Jude scrabble around in the drawer for the condom. Finding one, he brandished it triumphantly and she laughed as he grinned and tossed it on the bed. It landed near her hand which drew his gaze to her nudity and his grin faded as his eyes took a very thorough tour, lingering on her nipples and the patch of hair at the apex of her thighs.

"Jesus, Clementine." His gaze flicked up to her face. "You're gorgeous."

His praise went to her head and other parts of her body. Considering he'd been with some seriously beautiful woman, how could it not?

She quirked an eyebrow. One of them in this room was decidedly more clothed. "Am I going to have to guess what you look like?"

Busy with a second tour of her body, he didn't reply. Heat flushed everywhere under the intensity of those eyes.

"Shall I…" Clem ran her hand from her waist to her hip and lower. "Start without you?" Because while having Jude look at her like he wanted to lick every inch of her was hot, it was *not* the same thing as him *actually* licking every inch of her.

His glittering gaze cut from the trail of her hand to her face. "No fucking way," he muttered, his voice all low and growly.

Then his shirt was up and off and his zipper being

97

yanked down was loud in the quiet of the house. He removed his jeans and his underwear in record time until he was standing before her without a stitch of clothing and it was Clem's turn to stare.

She thanked god for the bleed of light around the pulled blinds falling softly in all his dips and hollows and showcasing all his hardness.

Holy. Cow. Jude was hot.

Chest, abs, thighs… And hanging between those thighs? Or *not* hanging as the case might be… yep, he'd filled out *well*.

It had been obvious even with his clothes on, that the scrawny boy had matured very nicely, but *this* sight? He was a veritable smorgasbord of honed masculine flesh, not a spare inch of fat to be found. He either didn't eat his food or he should definitely donate his metabolism to science after he was gone.

"Wow," she said on a whoosh of breath.

Not the most articulate thing to say but complex sentences were beyond her right at the moment. She picked up the condom and passed it to him. "On."

He chuckled. "How about we take some time before we get down to it?"

Nope. That wasn't going to work for her. All the reasons they shouldn't do this had fled a long time ago. Her mind was made up. All she needed now was the mattress at her back and Jude at her front. Jude inside her, holding her, taking her far away from the things that had played on repeat this past week.

"If you think I want to wait for you to put that"—she

YOU HAD ME AT CHOCOLATE

pointed to his erection, sprouting hard and perfect from a thatch of dark, red hair at its base—"in me for one second longer than I have to, then you are badly underestimating how much I need this right now."

He regarded her for a moment or two and Clem wondered if she'd put her foot in it. Was her directness as off-putting to him as braces had been to Billy Marsh? She knew Jude's reputation. She wouldn't have thought he'd have a problem with boldness—unless it was coming from little Clem Jones.

But then he reached over and plucked the condom out of her fingers with a, "Yes ma'am," and Clem watched him apply the latex sheath. He was quick and efficient, rolling it down, *handling* himself in a way that was seriously revving her already overheated system.

Job complete, he lifted his head and their eyes met.

Crooking her finger she said, "Come here."

Putting a knee on the mattress, he prowled toward her on all fours like a massive jungle cat ready to pounce—ready to *mate*—and Clem's pulse fluttered wildly at her temples and in her throat. It belted behind her rib cage and throbbed between her legs. She rolled onto her back as he planted a hand either side of her shoulders then lowered himself slowly, his body settling on top of hers.

Clem welcomed the press of him, good and big and sol-id, pining her to the mattress and she moaned and shut her eyes as his dick slid with precision through the slick heat between her legs. When she opened her eyes a beat later, they were joined from thighs to ribs, their upper torsos separated slightly as he supported himself on the flats of his forearms

99

resting either side of her head.

His hands came up to smooth her curls as he stared at her intently. "What do you suppose our eight-year-old selves would have thought if they'd known that one day we'd be doing this?" he asked, his voice husky.

Clem smiled. "They'd have been pretty grossed out."

He chuckled and it bathed her in goose bumps. "Fourteen-year-old me wouldn't have been."

"Oh yeah, what would he have thought?"

"I don't know. But it would have involved a hefty degree of masturbation, I imagine."

She blinked at his frankness then laughed and he did too, dropping his face to the crook of her neck. Warm puffs of his breath set her skin alive and hardened her nipples. As if he could feel the diamond points, his laughter quietened then stopped and he started to nuzzle, setting her entire body aflame.

From the pulse throbbing in her neck to the hollow at the base of her throat and the long ridge of a collarbone, Jude mapped her skin with his mouth. Waves of heat undulated to all her erogenous zones making her moan his name until he claimed her lips again in long, drugging kisses that had her twining her arms around his neck and arching into his body.

His kisses consumed her. They filled up her head, pushing out the anxiety and the worry. They soothed and gentled even as the steady rhythmic rock of his hips pulsed his cock through the slick folds of her sex, turning up the heat, cranking the tension behind her belly button.

"Jude," she muttered against his mouth as she reached

between their bodies, grabbing for him, needing the full thrust of him. "Please. I need you in me."

But he evaded her hands. "Hold that thought." He dropped a brief kiss on her mouth. "I'll be back in a bit."

And he kissed down again. Down, down, down. Trekking between her breasts to her navel and lower still, his end goal apparent.

"Jude." She plowed her hand into his hair and gave a gentle pull. "Come back here."

He lifted his head, his gaze meeting hers. "You don't like it?"

She gave a half laugh at the disappointment stamped across his features. "I love it. I just need *more* right now."

Dropping a kiss on her belly he smiled. "*Ohhh*, you need some dick, huh?"

His frank language only fanned the flames of her desire. "I really, *really* do," she admitted, her hand sliding from his hair.

And that was what he gave her, kissing quickly up her body again to her mouth, claiming it in a slow, deep possession that stole her breath as he eased between her legs. His *dick* nudged her entrance, pausing for only a beat before sliding home, stealing her breath all over again.

"Oh *god*," she muttered on a sharp exhalation, squeezing her eyes shut as he stretched her all the way to the hilt. Her pulse was like a waterfall in her head, her breathing like a jet engine. "There… just there… just like that."

"Yes," he agreed, his voice rough. "*Yes.*"

Slowly he withdrew before gliding back in again with a muffled kind of groan and Clem cried out as she lifted to meet his entry. A tug of sensation flared to life as the action pulled down on just the right spot. "Don't stop, please don't stop."

"I won't," he assured on a ragged exhalation.

And he didn't. He just withdrew and entered in the same inexorable fashion, his shoulders hunching as he rose over her with every push of his hips, the big blades in his back moving beneath the clutch of her palms. The flare grew hotter and hotter and bigger and bigger, spreading to her ass and her thighs and the muscles that held him locked inside her.

"God… Jude…" Clem grabbed for breath as her orgasm fizzed like a rocket before takeoff. She snatched at the heated air surrounding them, dragging it in to her starved lungs as everything melted down and the pleasure let fly.

There was nothing gentle about the orgasm, her internal muscles clamping hard on his cock as her ankles locked hard around the backs of his thighs. "Oh… god… *Juuuude*."

"Yes." He groaned right into her ear. "*Yes.*"

And then his back bowed and his breath cut off and his hips snapped to a sudden halt as he gasped her name and just held her for a beat, his huge body shuddering with his release before resuming the rock of his hips, riding them through the tumult of their orgasm all the way to the very, very end.

Until it winged away leaving them spent.

Clem floated like a dust mote in the aftermath, hovering through a haze of warm incandescent light, falling and twirling, dipping and rising, until the pillow of air finally evaporated delivering her gently to earth. Her limbs were heavy and her eyes were heavy and every cell she owned was

YOU HAD ME AT CHOCOLATE

drowned in fatigue.

Slowly, she became aware of Jude collapsed on top of her, of his lips at her neck, of the fan of his breath and the erratic belt of his heart through the wall of his chest.

Of the erratic belt of *hers*.

He shifted then, easing away, slipping from her body. A protest rose in Clem's throat but he hushed her, scooping her against his side and she snuggled in, her head settling into the crook of his neck.

"That was nice," she murmured, her lips barely moving. Because it had been. More than that it had been *exactly* what she'd needed.

His low chuckle, the press of his lips on her forehead, and his whispered, "Good night, Clementine," were the last things she was conscious of as she succumbed to sleep.

A STREAK OF trepidation shot through Clem as she entered the kitchen the next morning at nine. She was showered and dressed in jeans and a sweater. She'd already spoken to her father. Her mom had had a restful night and had woken to a little more movement down her left side, which the doctors thought was promising and had put her mom in good spirits.

She just hoped Jude was in good spirits, too. And that she hadn't blown things between them because of the sex. She'd hate to have to regret something that had been *that* good.

And it wasn't like she'd planned it.

But being with Jude last night had felt like old times and

they'd slipped into that easy rapport, which had been the hallmark of their friendship, and then he'd mentioned kissing and her brain had fritzed out a little.

"Morning," she said, injecting a bright note into her voice. Teaming it with an equally bright smile, she entered to find him in jeans and a T-shirt, putting a tray in the oven. The kitchen smelled sweet and yeasty and fluffy croissants were cooling on the island counter.

He turned and his face warmed and his mouth kicked up into a smile and he said, "Hey." And it was low and sweet and so sexy Clem actually went a little weak below the belly button.

Of course, he hadn't *meant* it to be sexy, she knew that but, hubba-*freaking*-hubba, Jude sure could pump out the pheromones.

"Sleep well?" he teased.

Clem blushed. "Sorry 'bout that, I guess I conked." But she did sleep well and this morning she felt utterly rested. *Replenished.* Ready to face another tough day at the hospital with her mom. And be there for her father.

"Yep."

He laughed as he stashed the tea towel through his belt loop and Clem thought—do not stare at that part of his anatomy. If she didn't want things to be awkward then she definitely shouldn't be staring at his dick.

Leaning his ass against the counter opposite, he folded his arms. "You were out like a light."

Her cheeks warmed some more and she placed her palms over them. "God, I'm so sorry. I'm usually better company after—"

Clem halted abruptly. After what? After sex? After doing the wild thing? After sleeping together? Making love. Oh Jesus—*no. Do* not *say that, idiot.*

Lordy. This was way harder than she'd imagined. Although, to be fair to herself, she'd had nowhere near the amount of one-night stand practice as Jude—if social media could be believed. He was, after all, her first.

His smile grew wider clearly amused at her discombobulation. "It's fine. You obviously needed it."

She had. But using him for what had essentially been a sleeping pill seemed mercenary in the cold light of day.

"You hungry?"

Clem leapt at the change of subject. "I am if those croissants are on offer."

"They are. And they should be cooled down enough to eat." He pulled the towel out from his belt and picked one up off the tray. Satisfied they were ready he put it on a plate for her and handed it over. "Coffee?"

Clem nodded and he turned to the coffee machine as she leaned her hip into the central bench. Man, he was good at this morning-after stuff, making it as easy and un-awkward for her as possible despite her ineptness. He wasn't pushing and he wasn't acting all freaked out. Just, business as usual.

But... as much as she'd like to pretend nothing had happened, the mature thing was to talk about it—make sure they were okay. That he was okay with staying just friends. Because she very much wanted *that*. Even if she'd never forget how good he looked naked. Or how tender and generous he was as a lover.

Placing her plate down on the nearby bench, she addressed his back. "I think we should talk about last night." She cleared the slight tremor in her voice betraying how high the stakes suddenly felt. "Make sure we're both on the same page."

Because there was a lot going on right now and although her life plans were on hold for the foreseeable future, it didn't mean she was abandoning them. Just putting them on pause. She still had her sights on a life outside Marietta.

He turned again, a lopsided smile on his face, his hands loose by his sides. "We can do that, if you want. Or, we can acknowledge that you've had a tough week and you needed to not think about it for a while." He shrugged. "I've been there. It was very clear last night that this was a one-off and I'm fine with that. I know you have plans for the next few years of your life. I'm just really happy to be back in it again. As a friend." He picked up her plate and thrust it at her again. "Eat. Relax. Go see your mom. Tell her and your dad I said hi. I cooked some more brownies and made up some leftovers from last night's dinner to take as well."

Clem blinked. "You did?" God... this man. How did she get so lucky?

"Unless—" He quirked an eyebrow. "You want to psychoanalyze every single second? I can do that."

Oh, *dear god*, no. Clem all but recoiled from the thought. Not least of all because if they picked over every kiss, touch, and caress from last night they might end up back in bed together and that would make it hard to sell the whole one-off thing.

"Nope." She shook her head. "I'm good."

Then she bit into the flaky pastry and forgot everything

as it crumbled on her lips and flooded her tastebuds with salty, buttery flakiness. She shut her eyes to savor it and, for a moment, forgot where she was and who she was with and actually *moaned*, it was that good.

"This croissant is..." She opened her eyes to find him staring at her, at her mouth, where her tongue was busy licking off pastry flakes. "Incredible."

His nostrils flared as his gaze tracked the flick of her tongue and Clem's stomach clenched at the streak of undiluted hunger in his eyes before he turned abruptly away and fiddled with the coffee. "It should be. I've made enough of them over the last ten years."

Breathing out slowly, Clem collected herself. It was only natural that they might still be a little caught up in their chemistry from last night, right? And a few days away at her mother's bedside should definitely see to that. She cast around for something to start that separation *now*. "So... what's on your agenda today?"

"I got a call from Edwin about an hour ago." He turned back, passing over a cup brimming with milky coffee, handle first. She took it with her spare hand and watched as he settled his ass back against the counter, folding his arms again, the hunger in his gaze gone.

Like it had never been there.

"Oh?" Clem inhaled the rich aroma of the beans as she blew on the heavenly brew. Her love affair with coffee had started during many a late-night session cramming for exams in college and she'd been addicted ever since.

"He wants me to come and see him at the Graff. I think he might have another wedding cake for me."

"Oh god." She grimaced. "Sorry about that." Although it had been inevitable that such a masterpiece would be noticed.

"It's okay. It was good to do something creative again and it'll give me a project while I look for a property with inn potential."

"How's that going?"

Clem realized these were the kind of questions she should have been asking him last night over dinner instead of unloading all her *stuff* on his shoulders. She'd really been all about herself last night and that didn't sit well because Clem had always put others before herself. It was how she'd ended up going stagnate in Marietta—putting everyone else's expectations of her ahead of her own desires and ambitions.

"I'm meeting with the Realtor this afternoon to look at some properties out of town."

"Oh." Clem's eyebrows raised. "That's exciting."

"I've seen a couple already. They just haven't quite been what I'm after."

"What *are* you after, exactly?"

He smiled. "I'm not really sure. I guess I'll just know it when I see it."

She sipped on her coffee. "Fair enough."

"You're heading to Bozeman after this?"

"Yeah. I need to go and check on a few things at the house for Dad first but then I'll hit the road."

"You're staying there the night?"

Clem tried hard not to think about tonight as it only led to thoughts of *last* night. But, given their deliciousness, they were bound to stick around. Which might well be a very good nightly distraction if her mother's recovery was slow or did not go according to plan. "I will, yes. I'll probably spend most nights there until Mom comes back to Marietta for rehab."

"I'm sure your dad will appreciate the support."

"Yeah… it was fortuitous the stroke happened when it did. I mean, not that I wanted it to happen at all," she assured hastily. Clem would give anything for this *not* to have happened to her mom. "But it did. And if I'd been living in New York…"

She shuddered at the logistics. Having to quit her job and move back home for a while. Which she would have done—*absolutely*. But there was no denying this timing was better.

He nodded slowly. "So, they said it could be a few weeks for your mom? Before she's well enough for rehab?"

"Uh-huh." It was strangely gratifying to know that Jude had actually listened to her last night as she'd unloaded. So many of her friends complained that their male partners never listened. "If all goes well. But, everyone is different blah-blah-blah." She sighed. "It's not even been a week since the stroke so the medical team is kinda guarded in their outlook."

"I guess they don't want to get ahead of themselves or give false hope."

"No." Clem shook her head. "In my brief experience with them, stroke doctors seem to be very cautious when talking to their patients and families."

"That's their job, I suppose. But it doesn't mean *you* can't be positive right? Be heartened by every forward step.

Your mom will need people like that around her, too."

"That's very true." Clem had got so caught up in her stroke research and worrying about all the what-ifs that she hadn't thought perhaps what her mom needed most was a cheerleader.

"You up for it?"

"Absolutely."

Clem was thankful again for the timing. Being free to be at her mother's bedside and be there for her dad—who also needed her right now—was a gift. Sure, the outpouring of support from the Marietta community had been immense but it would be her and her dad at the front line every day so a positive attitude was a must.

"Good." He nodded. "And I'll feed you so well you can't help but be positive."

Clementine laughed. "I will hold you to that, buddy."

Their gazes clashed briefly as the knowledge of how they'd stepped over that buddy line hovered between them but then Jude chuckled and the moment passed.

"I'll talk to the Realtor this afternoon about speeding up the process for finding me a rental so I'm not under your feet when you get back to Marietta. I might even see what's around to buy, could be easier in this tight rental market."

"No." Clem shook her head adamantly. "It's fine. Please don't feel you have to go anywhere. Not until you've found what you really want. You won't be under my feet and I have a spare room."

The thought of him leaving had put a sudden itch up her spine. Especially if it was because of what happened last night. She couldn't blame him if it was so but she really hoped not.

"Of course, if you feel that you need to," she added, "after last night then—"

"I don't," he interrupted. "I'd like to. Stay. If you're okay with that?"

Clem nodded vigorously, the itch evaporating on a rush of relief. "I am."

"Good. Makes it a hell of a lot easier to cook for you."

He grinned then, big and sexy and rendering Clem a little breathless. Thankfully Jude's cell phone chose that moment to ring. Pulling it out of his back pocket, he glanced at the screen. "It's the Realtor. Sorry, I should take this."

"Of course." Clem waved him away as he hit the answer button and strode out of the kitchen with a swagger that stilled the breath in her lungs.

It was hard to believe less than a week ago, the last person on her mind had been Jude, her old childhood friend from summer camp. She thought about how their lives had diverged all those years ago only to end back together again with him being firmly square and center.

With his croissants and his inn and his apparent power to reach inside her chest and *stop her breath*. Clem didn't know what that said about the universe but she did know it wasn't something she wanted to ponder too closely.

Not after last night.

Chapter Six

JUDE WAS WAITING to cross Main Street on his way to the Graff half an hour later, the morning air still crisp, his breath fogging into the air. If he looked to his left he'd see Copper Mountain but he wasn't taking in any of the scenery—his mind was running the play on last night—*again*.

It had been… well, it had rocked his world.

After her initial wobble, Clementine had been bold and assertive and wonderful. And not afraid to ask for what she needed. Sure, he'd been with bold women before but they'd known he was a sure thing. Clementine hadn't. She'd been keeping him firmly in the friend zone and it had been a real risk to reach out the way she had, to open up like that.

And not just physically. She'd opened herself up *emotionally* last night. She'd been vulnerable to him and that was entirely different. In seeking intimacy with him, she'd bared a little of her soul.

Jude had slept with a bunch of different women and had found a bunch of different things in their arms. Sexual release, fun, laughter, good times. Also things like avoidance and escape. But what he'd found with Clementine had been something else entirely.

He'd found *sanctuary*. Like he was where he belonged.

After a tumultuous time in his life, he'd come to Marietta searching for what he thought was the missing piece. That missing piece had kicked his ass to the curb. But last night, he'd found something else. Something better. After years of feeling he didn't fit in anywhere—not at his mom's or his dad's or Paris or New York—he'd found home.

Holding Clementine, *being* with Clementine, had felt like home.

Which was a bit of a problem because he knew their surprise liaison hadn't meant the same thing to her. He'd known Clementine had only been looking for distraction. For something to quiet the worries and anxieties in her mind. To take her away for a few hours. To give her a night of sleep that was deep and restorative and not haunted by the *what-ifs* of her mother's stroke.

She'd been after a tranquilizer, and he'd had zero problems being what she'd needed.

But the truth was, *any* guy could have given her that. Hell, she probably could have found it via her own hand or with the help of a vibrator if she'd truly set her mind to orgasm therapy. But she hadn't.

She'd asked *him*.

And he was glad to have been a port in her storm. Glad they'd slept together. Because now he had a clarity that he'd not had before. Now he had a sense of *home*. Coming to Marietta might had been a whim, but he knew now he was meant to be here.

With or without Clementine in the picture, this road he was on felt *right*.

"Young man? Young man."

It took a second or two for the imperious voice to pierce Jude's concentration and realize he was being addressed. He turned to find a woman bringing up the rear, with a determination as steely as the gray threaded through her dark hair and a look that could pierce a flak jacket.

"Yes, ma'am?" he said, drawing to a halt.

She was a little out of breath by the time she pulled in next to him. "You're the guy who did Tamsin's wedding cake, aren't you?"

"That's right." He stuck out his hand. "Jude Barlow, ma'am. Pleased to meet you."

"Carol Bingley." She shook firmly and released. "I just wanted to let you know you did a good job at such short notice. It was very nice indeed."

Nice.

That word brought back another memory from last night. It had been the one Clementine had used in the aftermath of their climaxes. Ordinarily, it would have made him wince. Nice wasn't exactly complimentary for a guy. It was right up there with *pleasant*. But the way she'd come apart in his arms had left him in no doubt she'd been utterly fulfilled and he'd given her what she'd wanted most—oblivion.

So, if that was *nice*, he'd take it.

"Thank you." He smiled absently as he scrubbed his mind of inappropriate thoughts.

"I didn't watch your TV show but Taylor Sheenan, she's Clem's boss, or *was* her boss, I suppose. She said you trained in Paris."

"That's right."

"How *interesting*." Somehow, Carol Bingley made interesting sound like a bad thing. She gave a little sniff and continued. "I've never been myself, too many French people for my liking but, the Eiffel Tower looks magnificent."

Jude supressed a horrified laugh at her snobbery. "Yes, ma'am."

"You're living at Clem's house, aren't you?"

"Yes."

"It's terrible what's happened to poor dear Trina," she tutted. "I do hope she's recovering, well."

"She's… stable." Jude was suddenly wary at questioning that had taken on an almost salacious tone.

Carol dropped her head on her side and regarded him for long moments, pursing her lips. "You're the one who proposed to her, aren't you?"

"Yep." Right there in front of everybody.

"But she said no, right?"

He grimaced. "Uh-huh."

"And do you think it's appropriate to be living in her house after she rejected you?"

Jude blinked. Okay then. *This* was actually happening. Paris might well be full of French people but they were French people who minded their own damn business. No random busybodies pulling him up in the street to go all judgy on his ass.

His teeth ached to tell this woman to mind her own damn business but he took a steady breath instead. "It's just until I find a rental. It's okay," he assured with a smile, "we go way back."

"Be that as it may," she said with a stern glare. "This isn't

Paris. It's a small town, young man. People talk, you know?"

Oh yeah. He knew. He was pretty sure he was staring directly at *people* right now.

But she'd plowed on before Jude got a chance to answer. "She needs a good man in her life. The poor thing was heartbroken after Reuben and her split up last year."

Jude wasn't sure this was any of his business. He certainly didn't want to hear it from a gossip on the streets of Marietta. But if Carol *whatshername* thought for a second that Clementine needed a man in her life then she really didn't know the younger woman at all.

"She doesn't need another man using her and leaving. If you know what I mean."

Jude almost laughed out loud considering how thoroughly she'd used him night. "As I said," Jude assured through tight lips, "it's nothing like that." The last thing he wanted was the old harridan passing around more gossip about them. "Now, if you'll excuse me, I'm late for an appointment."

He didn't give her a chance to respond or wait for the signal to change to allow him to safely cross, he just turned away and strode across the road, anger propelling him all the way to the Graff. Taking a breath to shake off his irritation, he stepped into the plush lobby and headed directly for the kitchens looking for Edwin—another one of those *French people*.

They'd met last week when Jude had used the Graff kitchens for the wedding cake and he'd liked the man instantly. They hadn't talked a lot but, as a fellow chef, he'd understood the man immediately. Edwin was all about the food and that made them cut from the same cloth.

The kitchens were in that lull between breakfast and lunch when Jude entered. Spotlessly clean stainless-steel counter gleamed under the downlights as he greeted some of the staff he'd met last week before spying Edwin. The other man welcomed him enthusiastically and they exchanged pleasantries in French as Edwin ushered them outside to the coffee machine where he made them both espressos.

Indicating they should sit at the deserted bar, Edwin switched to impeccable English—way more impeccable than Jude's French—as he launched into his spiel.

"I know you're looking around for some property to open an inn and I gather that working is off your radar for the moment but I was hoping to interest you in doing some decorative work for me, which should only take an hour or so each day?"

Jude took a sip of his espresso. "I'm listening. Go on."

"I was impressed with the chocolate baskets you made for the individual cake slices at the wedding. It's obvious from watching some of your decorative flourishes on *Yes, Chef*—"

"You watched *Yes, Chef*?" Jude interrupted. It had been his experience that working chefs were not fond of TV chefs.

Edwin grinned. "I streamed the first season over the weekend and fast forwarded to your bits." Jude chuckled and Edwin continued. "You've clearly had a lot of experience with chocolate art and I'm wanting that extra something that can be added to the plate to really make our dessert menu stand out. The flashier and more intricate the better."

"Okay."

"There is a lot of culinary competition from Bozeman,

particularly as we come into this time of year with Halloween, Thanksgiving, the Marietta Stroll in the first week of December, and then Christmas, of course. The Graff has always prided itself on standing out. Something like zis—" His first hint at an accent. "Could make all the difference."

Jude liked the way the man thought. Food was about the eye as well as the stomach. "Surely you have someone on your staff who could perform that role for you?"

"My chefs can, of course, do basic stuff on the run but I'm looking for something spectacular. Something unique, with *wow* factor. Something that changes from day to day and will have tongues wagging. And when we clearly have a master in our presence then..." He shrugged. "Why not? Plus, it gets very busy in here with three food services a day so there's not a lot of time for flourish, no?"

Having worked in busy kitchens all his chef life, Jude understood that only too well.

"To have something premade earlier that day that can be pulled from the fridge and added to the plate would make everything so simple. Or even something that was individually made for a specific customer for a special celebration. That would be—" Edwin kissed his fingertips and blew a dramatic chef's kiss into the air. "Perfection." He sipped his espresso again. "You could come in whenever you wanted in the morning. Fit it in with your schedule and you can have your own work area and fridge."

Jude was tempted. He'd enjoyed the combination of creative and culinary outlet Tamsin's wedding cake had provided. "I'm interested." He nodded. "Keep talking."

"Good." Edwin grinned triumphantly. "Because there's

more." He downed the rest of his coffee in a quick swallow. "Come with me."

Jude quickly swigged his coffee down as Edwin vacated his stool and headed out of the restaurant. Catching up, they crossed the lobby to the gift store which had a glass front and was situated in a bit of a nook overlooking part of the lobby and the bar. It wasn't open yet but Jude could see shelves and tables boasting artfully displayed merchandise.

"Miranda Telford runs the Graff gift shop. She carries all kinds of things from the practical stuff guests might need, to food and gift items produced by local artisans. A little bit of Montana for our guests to take home with them."

"Uh-huh."

"I was talking to her yesterday about the possibility of a display table to feature the amazing chocolate artistry of the Graff's very own *chocolatier*. It would obviously be a much bigger canvas so you could be as elaborate as you'd like. Miranda themes the shop according to the season so you could possibly theme your displays, too?"

Jude nodded, already envisioning what he could do. He was no Madam Fontaine but he was no slouch, either. "That could work."

"Last year there was a hot chocolate competition in Marietta that spilled over into all the towns in the area, Bozeman included. I was thinking maybe we could get a little friendly rivalry going again this year between the towns? An overall grand prize for the town with the best chocolate displays as well as one for an individual display? I know Sage from Copper Mountain Chocolates and Viv from *Delish* would both be interested. I could source a chef from outside the area to be the judge but locals could also vote for their favorite displays?"

"That sounds like fun." Jude's competitive spirit kicked to life.

"So... is that a yes? Are you in?"

Jude nodded. "Preliminarily, yeah."

It was perfect, actually. It would give him something to do while he looked for a property. Jude was lucky enough to be in a very good financial position—in fact, if he was smart and managed his money well, he'd never have to work again—but he'd never been idle, and he didn't want to start. Plus, it would help him get to know people around town.

"Let's go back to the bar and you can talk to me about dining numbers and supply and the logistics of it all."

"Yes, Chef," Edwin said with a grin.

Jude rolled his eyes. Yeah, he'd not heard that one before....

THE NEXT THREE weeks alternated between days where things sped along and days that grinded slower than a wet month but, after four weeks in Bozeman, Clem was finally settling her mom in the Marietta hospital, where her intensive rehabilitation would commence.

Her mother had come a long way in a few short weeks. Her facial droop had all but disappeared and with it her speech had improved. It wasn't perfect and there were still some swallowing issues necessitating a feeding tube, but she was largely comprehensible, which had lessened frustrations considerably. Her balance had also improved despite still dealing with significant weakness in her left arm and leg which hindered her ability to mobilize and required substantial assistance.

As much as her mom wanted to go home and her father wanted to bring her home, she had been assessed as requiring the kind of support better accessed in a health care setting. Once she was mobilizing more reliably, able to protect her airway better and attend to her personal care needs, she could be discharged home to attend rehab on a continuing outpatient basis.

The doctors hadn't wanted to put any time frame on how long that might take but with the kind of intensive therapy she could get as an impatient they were hoping to see meaningful improvement over the next couple of months. They had been warned, though, that it would likely be much longer for a *complete* recovery and to prepare themselves for the possibility that there might always be some residual effects.

Cautiously suggesting Christmas as a discharge goal to work *toward*, her mom had not been impressed. She'd been adamant it would be Thanksgiving and when Trina Jones put her mind to something, she got it done.

Like mother, like daughter.

Clem was just pleased to see her mom was back to her fighting self. There had been days throughout the past weeks when she'd been so despondent Clem and her dad had despaired. It certainly had been hard to keep positive when Trina was either crying or angry. Her poor father, who had borne the brunt of his wife's dissatisfactions, had been beside himself with worry. To see the woman he loved in a whiplash-inducing Jekyll and Hyde act had been gut-wrenching for him and Clem knew he'd felt utterly helpless.

He was so used to being the one who fixed things but he couldn't fix this and it had taken an emotional toll.

"You head home now, darling," her father said, kissing her on the forehead. "I'll stay with Mom until after dinner."

Clem nodded, pleased that her mother's transfer to Marietta meant that her father would be back home, surrounded by people who knew and loved him and who could help out. One of Clem's first goals was to establish a roster of her mother's friends who could come to the hospital and keep Trina company, both for her own mental health, and to provide some regular respite for her dad.

"Thanks, Dad. Sleep well back in your bed for the first time in a month." He'd not been home overnight since the stroke and Clem knew he was looking forward to the comfort of his own mattress.

He gave her a weary kind of smile. "Oh, I will, don't you worry about that."

Clem squeezed his arm. She knew how he felt—tired down to her bones. From anxiety and too many days of emotional ups and downs and the mammoth effort it had taken to get her mom even this far. She kissed her mom's cheek. "See you tomorrow. It's so good to have you back in Marietta."

Her mother's smile was slightly lopsided but it was pure joy. "It's good to be home," she agreed, her speech slow and deliberate and a little slurred on the last word like it often got at the end of the day. It was perfectly intelligible, especially considering how difficult her speech had been at the start, but Clem could tell she was tired.

Happy for sure, but still tired.

CLEM DROVE THROUGH the streets of Marietta, along Main Street all decorated up for the season change and Halloween and she realized she'd practically missed *fall* cooped up in Bozeman hospital. And how many days was it until excited little trick or treaters were running around her street? She squinted trying to remember—Sunday! In two days!

Man, where had October gone?

She should have been on a Greek island—sun, sand, blue skies as far as the eye could see. Maybe not hot but not chilly either. No bare branches everywhere she looked, no pumpkins and cobwebs. For sure, there wasn't any other place Clem wanted to be right now but this whole episode had only reiterated how life could turn on a dime.

That it was finite. And there to be *lived*.

It was just after six and almost dark when Clem pulled up at the curb outside her house. Jude's sporty little SUV he'd bought two weeks ago sat in the drive like it had always been there and a plume of smoke twirled out of the chimney and her heart went *kerthump*.

She'd come home only sporadically these past weeks but knowing he was going to be there when she did, had been, well... lovely, even if they had been a bit like ships passing in the night. During the day, she rarely saw him and at night she often didn't get in until after ten. But there was always food to be had and a pot of coffee in the morning and knowing he was keeping an eye on things for her here had been one more weight off her mind.

Sure, she could have called on a dozen friends and neighbors for the same but the thought of him here in her house just... made her happy. Their friendship, which had once meant so much to her, was being reestablished—in spite of their little slipup—and she didn't realize how much she'd missed him until he'd come back into her life.

The aroma of woodsmoke scented the air as she walked up the path pulling her carry-on-sized bag behind her for the last time. The porch was bare and she made a mental note to do something about the state of it tomorrow or she'd be evicted from the neighborhood. Looking around the nearby houses she could see pots of bright colored mums, pumpkins of all shapes and sizes—some already carved—along with cornstalks and scarecrows decorating porches.

Not to mention witches, cobwebs, and skeletons.

Yep, tomorrow she'd do something about it but, for now, she just wanted to relax and enjoy knowing she didn't have to do that trip to Bozeman and back any time soon.

She let herself into the house which smelled like an Italian restaurant. Jude appeared in the kitchen doorway in his low-rider jeans and those damn bare feet. "Hey," he said and her heart went *kerthump, kerthump.*

Suddenly, the mortifying scald of hot tears burned at the backs of her eyes and she blinked them away furiously. She would *not* cry all over him again. "Hey, yourself."

He didn't ask if she was okay, he must have just sensed that she was a bit wobbly and he crossed the distance between them, holding out his arms as he got nearer. Clem melted into them gratefully, sighing as his big arms went around her and his chin came to rest on top of her head. She pressed her face to his chest, the steady thump of his heart a reassuring metronome beneath the blade of her cheekbone and it felt so damn good.

So *right*.

Right in a warm, fuzzy way. And right in a hot and heavy way as things stirred below her belly button. Which was all kinds of wrong. They'd had their one night and moved on. What she needed now was *not* hot and heavy, it was warm and fuzzy.

"Your mom settle in?" His words rumbled around his chest straight into her ear.

"Uh-huh." Her voice was muffled but she didn't care.

"Big day."

"Long."

"Momentous, too."

"Yep."

Clem swallowed against the lump in her throat. She felt like her mom had climbed a mountain and she and her dad had been walking beside her holding her up and, although there was still a way to go before they got to the summit, for the first time they could actually see it and her mom was standing on her own two feet.

And that wasn't nothing.

"You hungry?"

Laughing, Clem pressed her forehead to his sternum. "I wasn't until I smelled your food and now I am ravenous."

He chuckled and it enveloped her in a deliciously sonorous echo. "That's what I like. A woman who appreciates my cooking."

"Are you kidding?" She glanced up, her eyes meeting his. Jude had practically sustained her and her father all this time. And not quick and easy food but gourmet stuff—with garnishes! "I don't know what my dad and I would have done without it this past month."

And there she went again tears stinging her eyes.

If he saw, he didn't mention it, he just smiled and performed a brief, completely nonsexual nose rub that was a good reminder of her stipulation to be friends. Giving herself a mental shake, Clem cleared her throat and pulled out of his embrace. Because it was just too damn tempting.

He was just too damn tempting.

"My ass definitely appreciates it."

His lips twitched. "If you're fishing for compliments about your ass, I am far too gentlemanly to comment."

Clem gave a half laugh. "Fine." She sighed dramatically to keep the light mood going. "What *is* cooking?"

"Risotto. Chicken and mushroom."

Saliva flooded Clem's mouth. "Yummo."

"I took some round to your dad's place earlier so there was something for him when he got home. There should be enough for a couple of nights. I popped a few more meals in his freezer, too."

"Oh, Jude." Clem pressed her hand to her chest. She'd texted him a list of basics to stock her father's fridge with yesterday, which he'd done for her but this? This was above and beyond. "You didn't have to do that. Dad is actually quite a capable cook."

He shrugged. "Just to take the pressure off a bit."

"You're so sweet."

He quirked an eyebrow. "According to the *New York Times* food critic, I'm a culinary badass."

Clem laughed out loud. Maybe he had cultivated a certain persona due to the TV show and his New York restaurateur guise but here in Marietta he was the boy she'd always known and she had to grind her heels to the ground so she wouldn't walk back into his arms. He deserved way more than her mixed signals.

"Do I have time for a shower?"

"Yep."

"Great." She smiled. "See you in ten."

FIFTEEN MINUTES LATER, they were ensconced in front of the television in their places at either end of the couch, cradling steaming bowls of risotto topped with fresh basil and shavings of Gorgonzola cheese. The lights were off, the fire was on, and there was fifteen minutes until *Lord of the Rings* was about to start. The food was divine and Clem had to work hard to suppress her vocal appreciation.

"Where are you at with the property hunt?" she asked, needing to fill the silence so her brain wouldn't go to places it shouldn't.

"Still searching," Jude replied not looking up from his bowl. "I'm heading out again tomorrow." He took another mouthful of food, swallowing it and washing it down with a merlot he'd poured into both their glasses. Glancing across at her he said, "You want to come with me?"

Clem blinked—that sounded so much fun. *And* a total departure from how she'd spent her last four weekends. "I'd *love* to do that. I just have a bit of a day, is all. I gotta see Mom in the morning and I was going to go out to the Donnelly farm at some stage and get some pumpkins for the porch."

"That should work for me. I've got to go do chocolate stuff at the Graff in the morning and I can pick up the key from the Realtor any time. We can go in the afternoon and fit in the pumpkin picking then? Haven't done that in years."

"Sounds great," Clem said with a smile.

More than great. It sounded so damn normal after the ups and downs of the previous month it actually bordered on bliss.

Jude chatted a bit about some of the properties he'd seen as they ate and then the movie came on and Clem was so warm and cozy and full it wasn't long before her eyes started to drift. She fought it for a while but she was just too damn tired from everything that had happened since she'd gotten that phone call at JFK and she didn't bother fighting it any longer, wriggling down until she was lying on her side, her legs drawn up so they weren't encroaching on Jude's space, her head on the overstuffed arm.

"You'll get a crick in your neck." His voice drifted over her in a warm cloud.

"Just for a few minutes," she murmured.

Except she didn't wake until the next morning, deliciously warm, cocooned in a blanket, the earthy aroma of coffee tickling her nostrils, a pillow under her head.

IT WAS THREATENING to snow just after lunch as Jude pulled up his vehicle in the drive of an old house sitting in the middle of its bare, frigid block on a rural road not far from Livingstone. He'd bet the bank that, even in its heyday, it hadn't been particularly welcoming.

"It looks like it has possibilities," Clementine said from the passenger seat, her eyes traveling over the sagging building.

"Hmm," he said noncommittally.

The truth was with enough money and imagination—one he had loads of, the other he could buy—any place could be spruced up to be something special. But not every place felt special from the get-go. That came from the house's *spirit* and it was *that* he was looking for.

This place, he knew already, *didn't* have it.

"Uh-oh," she murmured. "That hmmm doesn't sound good."

Jude grinned. "It's my I'm reserving judgment hmmm."

"Whatever." Clementine rolled her eyes and opened the car door. "Just, keep an open mind, okay?"

"Yes, ma'am," Jude said with a resigned sigh as he got out of the car and they trailed across the block to the house. The clapboard was peeling and there was no porch, no steps, just a crumbling concrete path leading straight to the front door which was fiddly to unlock, requiring much jiggling and a muted cuss word or two.

It was as if it, too, was trying to discourage anyone from entering. Like Jude needed any more impetus...

Eventually, it ceded to his will and they entered. It was only marginally less frigid than outside and streams of their dragon breath frosted into the air as they wandered from one soulless room to the other. Clementine commented on the things that could be done to make it into the cozy inn of his dreams but all Jude could see was what it wasn't.

It wasn't *the one*. He didn't *feel* it in his gut.

They stood at the back window looking through the dirty pane, their warm breaths causing patches of fog on the glass. A sweeping view of brittle grass and nude trees stretched in front of them. Jude supposed in summer it would look very different but it was hard to imagine with winter bleaching the color from the landscape.

He couldn't even see a mountain which was no easy feat in this part of Montana. It looked about as inviting as an arctic tundra. He was surprised a tumbleweed hadn't blown across the yard.

"It needs a lot of work," he said because that at least sounded like he was *keeping an open mind*.

"You have the time and the money."

That was true but... "It feels cold."

She laughed. "It's about to *snow*, Jude."

He glanced at her sheepishly. "You know what I mean."

"No." She shook her head. Her curls were tucked into a knitted cap with kitten ears that she apparently got in Budapest last year and made her look cute as hell. Her nose was red tipped and those cute chipmunk cheeks were rosy. "I don't know if I do. What *are* you after? A new build, a renovation? How many rooms? You want to live on site or hire a manager?"

"I'm happy to renovate and I'd prefer an older place with a bit of history to it." Pulling elements out of his head to assemble a vision was harder than he'd bargained. "Something smallish just a few rooms upstairs and an extra one for me to live on site. Definitely a big old dining room and a wraparound porch and some land with trees to climb. A great big farmhouse-style kitchen. I want to make good, hearty meals for my guests. Chowders and cobbler and pot roast and corn bread. Traditional food, the stuff from yesteryear. The kind that fills bellies and makes memories and brings people back because sitting at my table made them happy."

"That sounds lovely."

Yeah. It was. Caught up in memories, Jude leaned his hands on the frigid wood of the windowsill but he barely felt the cold as he stared out over the uninviting landscape, the complete antithesis of his dream property.

"For one week a year—the *same* week every year—Mom and Dad and I would fly into Houston then drive to the inn near Rockport and Dad would watch his migrating cranes all day and Mom got to bake in the sun at the beach and they were so damn happy. No sniping, no arguments. No loaded silences. They actually laughed and it felt like we were a family again. That's what I want. The kind of place that families want to return to, year after year."

She already knew about the little inn. He'd told her about it the first day they'd met. It was why she'd folded paper cranes for him every camp. Because she'd thought having a bird-watching dad was pretty cool instead of weird like his friends.

A hand slipped onto his shoulder. "You're probably not going to find a replica of the place you stayed at in Texas, Jude." Her palm was warm and her voice was gentle and Jude shut his eyes against the pull of both. "This is Montana after all."

Sure, he knew that. But it wasn't about replicating an architectural style.

"It's not about what it looks like," he dismissed, opening his eyes as he turned to face her, displacing her hand. "You have to feel it here." He slapped his belly.

He'd never really felt that about *Hey Jude*—he'd been guided by what others thought was a good look and a good location and a good *vibe* and he had been proud of it, but it had never given him that warm and fuzzy feeling he'd gotten as a kid. Of course, a hip New York restaurant and a tiny Texan inn couldn't be compared but, deep down, Jude had always craved the latter.

"But... isn't that what *you* create?" Her question was earnest her eyebrows beetling together. "Isn't that about people? People make a house and home. People make an inn a home away from home. That's what *you* bring to the table, right? *You* set the tone, *you* create the vibe. Like that woman who ran the inn and taught you how to cook apple cobbler?"

"Mrs. Ledbetter," he supplied, smiling once again at her memory. "Yeah... she'd have probably made any place welcoming especially with the aromas that always emanated from her kitchen. She used to say to me, 'Food is home, Jude. Food is love,' and she poured her heart and soul into everything she cooked."

"Right." Clementine nodded. "*You're* the *X* factor."

"Yeah, but she also told me that she'd fallen in love with the house at first sight and it had broken the bank—they were her exact words—but she had to have it anyway."

"And that's what you're after?"

"Yup." And he was *not* lacking in funds.

She glanced out the window again giving the view a disparaging once-over. "And this isn't it, is it?"

"Nope." He shook his head emphatically. "It's not the one."

Regarding him for a beat or two, she pursed her lips. "Might it be possible," she asked quietly, tentatively, "that you're stalling? 'Cause you're scared it'll all come tumbling down again and you want this too much?"

Jude grimaced as he recognized elements of truth in Clementine's amateur analysis. He grunted. "You charge by the hour for this?"

"Should I?" She quirked an eyebrow. "How'd I do?"

"Not bad for an amateur. You forgot about my yearning for roots that stems from the long-term psychological impact of parental discord and divorce."

Her lips twitched. "That'll all be in my report."

"Along with your bill, I suppose?"

"First session is free."

He chuckled. "Come on, Clementine Jones." Jude pushed away from the depressing view. "Let's go get us some pumpkins."

Chapter Seven

JUDE SLOWED THE car as he approached a farm gate with a display of pumpkins and pots of vibrant mums artfully arranged on either side.

"I've been thinking," Clementine said as he indicated to turn into Donnelly's farm.

Jude glanced across at her as he waited for the line of oncoming traffic to pass. Her brow was scrunched in concentration below the band of the kitten-eared cap. He laughed, he couldn't help himself.

"What?" she demanded.

He shook his head, his attention now on the road. "You look adorable in that hat."

"I know," she said batting her eyelashes.

He laughed again and wished he wanted to ruffle her hair or tweak her nose like a little sister instead of lean over and kiss the hell out of her mouth. As much as he tried to friend zone her, he couldn't deny his physical attraction to Clementine.

"I could do some research for you, if you like?"

"What kind of research?" he asked as he turned into the property and drove slowly through the gate.

"You were saying you wanted to cook traditional food

and it got me thinking. I could do a search on recipes that they used a long time ago. At inns or saloons, particularly in this area. Ones that might have fallen out of popularity. We also have such a rich indigenous history, I could search for Native American recipes. I know you won't be thinking about menu items for ages but it might be kinda cool to feature a couple of dishes with traditional roots both European and indigenous? It could be a real selling point?"

A warm glow flared to life in the center of Jude's chest as he followed the slow-moving car in front down the tree-lined drive, absently noting the bare branches poking toward the leaden sky. He glanced across at her. "Really?"

"Sure." She smiled. "I'm a librarian—that's what we do. It's not all standing behind a desk checking out books and scolding people to be quiet."

He chuckled trying not to think about Clementine in a twinset, her hair in a bun, peering over the glasses perched on the end of her nose as she scolded him.

Clearing his throat—and his filthy mind—he said, "That's such a great offer, thank you. But... I don't want to take time away from your mom."

"I'll have more time now that she's in Marietta and it'll give me something to do. Plus, I love research."

"I remember. You used to send me those factoids about the multitude of crane species in your letters."

She grinned. "That was fun."

The glow in Jude's chest intensified and he found it difficult to breathe for a moment. Being attracted to Clementine was one thing but this feeling was deeper than that. Deeper than friendship, too, and that was veering into dangerous territory. "Okay, how about this?" he suggested, desperate to get on an even footing. "I could pay you. As a research assistant."

Jude congratulated himself on the idea. Money was a sure-fire way to kill *feelings* and, as she'd briefly mentioned last week that was what her job in New York involved, it was perfect. Plus, this way he could compensate her for putting him up rent free.

"Absolutely not." She shook her head. Her response was vehement but not angry.

"I'm good for it you know," he teased. "And you should be paid for something like this."

He wasn't sure what her financial situation was but she obviously had enough to tide her over until she started in New York, because he couldn't imagine her not planning for that. Unless she'd been factoring in the sale of her house, which had been put on hold.

"Don't be a dork. You've been a personal chef to me and Dad for the last month. I imagine something like that costs a bomb out in the real world. Consider it payback."

He laughed at the dork as he turned into the parking area. "No way. I'm living in your house rent free and it's been a pleasure to cook for you guys." Jude turned into the parking area. "I don't need payback."

"And neither do I. It will be my pleasure to research for you. Seriously, I'm kinda excited about it to be honest."

She bounced a little in his peripheral vision, the streak of anticipation in her voice was a mile wide. He laughed again and shook his head. "*Dork.*"

"Yes, sir." She shot him an unashamed grinned. "That's

me."

Alighting the vehicle a minute later, they joined what appeared to be half of Marietta in the farm shop. Everyone greeted Clementine with such warmth as they wandered past stands bursting with produce from buckets of apples and ears of corn to pots of mums and, of course, pumpkins.

It was clear her mom was much loved as people stopped to ask after her, eager for an update from Clementine. Sensing his superfluousness *and* the speculative gazes coming his way, Jude left her to it and set about grabbing a variety of different produce, holding the different pumpkins up for Clementine's approval. She nodded or shook her head but didn't stop chatting.

Once he had a dozen of varying sizes, as they'd discussed on the trip to the farm, he had grabbed some mums and some apples—tarte tatin for dinner tonight—and paid for the purchases taking them to the car and loading them into the trunk. Clementine was still talking to a small gathering of women when he was done although her smile was looking more polite now than appreciative and when she glanced at him her eyes definitely telescoped a *get me out of here* message.

Jude was totally up for that job.

"Excuse me, ladies," he said, sweeping in and interrupting the conversation. "But I need Clementine."

That sure stopped the conversation in its tracks as five women stared at him owlishly. Clementine pressed her lips together clearly trying to stop herself from laughing.

"I have a jack-o'-lantern dilemma only she can help me with." He held out his hand and she took it with a demure,

"Excuse me everyone," her eyes sparking with humor.

It wasn't until they were outside and walking toward the pumpkin fields that Clementine let go of his hand with a laugh. "That was very wicked. They're going to think we're a couple now."

Jude shrugged as nonchalantly as he could as the thought wormed into his brain. "Let them. We know the truth."

They were friends. Just friends. Jude figured if he said it often enough he'd talk himself into it. Or at least put those *feelings* firmly back in their place.

"Says a guy who's spent years living in enormous cities." She shook her head. "Anyway... let's get the biggest pumpkin we can and make the entire street jealous of our jack-o'-lantern."

Grateful for a change in topic, his competitive nature spurred to life. "I am for that."

They approached a guy who looked to be in his seventies. Jude assumed he was the farmer as Clementine called him by name. "Winston, we want your biggest, fattest, orange-est pumpkin," she declared.

The older man's smile was big and wide. "I got just the one, Clem. Follow me."

TEN MINUTES LATER with a monster pumpkin on board Jude turned his vehicle back onto the road heading home.

Home. How was it that in a month, Clementine's house felt more like home than the East Village loft he'd lived in for five years? That he looked forward to decorating the porch almost as much as he did the friendly waves from neighbors as he walked to the Graff every morning.

"Thanks for today," she said with a sigh. "It felt so normal after the past month."

"Good." Jude glanced across at her to find her looking at him. The air vents blew out a steady stream of heat and her hat and scarf had been removed and she was all loose and relaxed in the seat. He smiled at her before turning his attention back to the road. "I'm glad."

"You're not like the *Yes, Chef* Jude at all, are you?" she mused.

The intensity of her gaze was like a brand on his profile and Jude's hands tightened around the wheel. "No."

"You're just like the boy I remember."

She said it so wistfully, it grabbed big handfuls of his guts and squeezed. "I've always been him," he said. "He just kind of got caught up in the spin and celebrity of a television show. Then started to believe some of his own press."

"I suppose it would be hard not to."

It was generous of her to give him an out but he'd brought a lot of his downfall on himself. "It *was* hard, actually. I could feel myself becoming this arrogant version of myself but didn't seem to be able to stop. Reality TV is a strange beast, they edit and manipulate footage until suddenly you're appearing one way and they really push it, especially if it becomes popular with the viewers. So it becomes a self-fulfilling prophecy with you behaving the way they've cultivated because you want to be popular, you *have* to be popular to win and the more outrageous the better because that's good for ratings, right?"

Even now, a year after getting away from the person he'd become thanks to *Yes, Chef,* echoes of that time persisted.

"And no one pulls you up on it," he continued, staring at the road ahead, his mood suddenly as bleak as the weather. "Lotta yes people around stroking your ego, telling you you're right and everyone else is the problem while they stuff your pockets full of money and promises and endorsements. And you can't stop, you can't take a break, you can't want to slow down because you can't be a quitter. Not when so many people, so many great chefs out there, wanted what I had. I couldn't squander that, I had to keep going."

"I'm sorry."

Her hand landed on top of his on the steering wheel. It was fleeting but it brought him back from that time and his knuckles relaxed. Hell, his *body* relaxed. "It's fine. I had a privileged life, I shouldn't be complaining."

She shrugged. "A gilded cage is still a cage, Jude."

There was such a depth of understanding in her tone, like Clementine knew all about gilded cages. "Is that how you felt in Marietta? Trapped?"

"No, not trapped. Just… stagnating. I'd been perfectly happy here, living the life I'd wanted since I was a little girl. Working hard at a career I loved, seeing a nice guy. But thirty was looming and I started to feel… I don't know… unsettled? Then a librarian friend of mine got a job at the Met in New York and another friend got breast cancer and I realized I hadn't really *lived* and that it was okay to want something different at almost thirty than I did at eight."

"Changing the status quo isn't always easy."

"Nope. My mom wasn't impressed." She stared out the

window. "I worry that maybe… my mom was fit and healthy… maybe the stress of me moving away played some part in the stroke."

"What?" Jude threw her an alarmed look. Had she been blaming herself for this? "No. Clementine… don't do that. Strokes happen to fit and healthy people, too." Yeah, he'd done a bit of googling. "You can't put that on yourself."

"I know. God, I think I could write a thesis on all that I've learned about strokes recently." She shook her head as if to clear it of her guilt-laden thoughts. "Ignore me." She turned to look at him. "Talk to me about Africa. You said it helped?"

Jude nodded going with her change of subject. "It took me a while to unwind, to shed the Jude I'd been conditioned to be. But, yeah… looking around I realized how far up my own ass my head had been. How much I *had* compared to these people who lived in this incredibly beautiful, incredibly raw, incredibly hard country."

"What did you do exactly? Where were you situated?"

"All around central Africa." It was hard to believe on this freezing, Montana day surrounded by low, dark skies, brittle gray branches and towering, snow-capped mountains, that six weeks ago he'd been in the sweltering heat surrounded by dry earth, vast swathes of ravaged land, and about a million flies. "I was part of a volunteer not-for-profit that worked on various construction projects in villages from wells to housing."

"You… built stuff?"

Jude honked out a laugh at the rich vein of disbelief in her voice. "What, I don't look like a construction worker?"

"I picture you more in an apron than a tool belt."

He was quite at home in both but that wasn't the important part of her statement. "So..." He quirked an eyebrow. "You picture me, huh?" With another woman this might have been considered flirting, but it wasn't. It was teasing. He and Clementine had always teased each other.

"Ha! You wish."

When their laughter settled he said, "I did help out where I could, actually. I can wield a hammer and work a screwdriver and know when to get out of the way. But my role was to cook. Volunteers need to be fed. In down times I sometimes ran basic, informal cooking classes for anyone from the village who wanted to join in using whatever was available locally which could sometimes be a real challenge. At one of the first villages there was a woman who taught at the school who saw me folding a paper crane and she asked if I'd come and teach the kids so I did and they loved it."

"I bet they did."

"I did the same from then on at all the schools if the teachers were interested. I started ordering origami paper by the truckload to come in with supply deliveries." He smiled remembering all the happy faces when their creation finally came together.

"Sounds like you enjoyed teaching?"

"I enjoyed all of it. More than that I think I... needed it." He glanced across at Clementine who was angled slightly toward him in her seat. "I needed to get out of my own head. My own ass, for sure." He smiled ruefully. "The whole experience was humbling and enriching. Transformative, I guess. I knew I couldn't go back to the way things had been.

Living there for a year, with people who had *so* little—by western standards anyway—taught me I didn't need any of the *stuff* I thought I did and seeing how tight-knit these communities were, despite their struggles, made me realize how... disconnected I'd been. I just hadn't figured out what I was going to do to change that in my life before my time was up."

"Which is how you ended up in Marietta on bended knee."

Jude gave a self-deprecating laugh. "Yeah, I was kinda panicked when I left Africa without a specific direction considering how much clarity I'd gained there. Apparently knowing what you don't want is the easy part. Knowing what you *do* want is a lot harder."

"Gosh," she said, one eyebrow lifted, laughter in her voice. "Who knew?"

"Yeah, yeah, smart-ass. I made a wild leap." It didn't make any sense looking at it now but it had seemed logical enough at the time. "But, I reckon the universe must have known something that I didn't, because the timing's been good as far as your mom's stroke goes. And I love the town, the area. I love how far away it is from New York. I love tinkering away at the Graff."

"Yeah." Her cheek rested against the headrest and a smile warmed her face. She looked happy and relaxed and Jude itched to slide his hand on her knee. Not anything sexual, just... companionable. "Everything's fallen in place, hasn't it?"

"It has."

"I'm pleased you came."

"Oh really?" He laughed because it suddenly felt very warm and intimate inside the car. His body aware of hers in ways that weren't remotely *companionable*.

"I missed you."

Jude's hands tightened around the wheel and he forced himself not to look at her. Not now when her voice was streaked with nostalgia and she was looking at him and talking to him like he was that boy he'd once been, not the man he now was.

The man who'd seen her naked. Who, as much as he knew there wasn't going to be a repeat, would very much like to see her naked again.

He'd been a fool to ever let their relationship flounder. Okay, it might not have grown into a sexual thing and it might still have fallen by the wayside as he'd risen to fame—or infamy, as the case might be—but if nothing else, he could have done with her pragmatism. Her counsel.

He swallowed. "I missed you, too."

"Let's not do that again," she said. "Let's not drift apart, again."

He nodded, still keeping his gaze firmly fixed on the road ahead. "Deal."

CLEM COULDN'T BELIEVE what a difference twenty-four hours could make. Her porch had been transformed. It looked like the Halloween fairy had thrown up but, hey, that was the way she liked it. There were pumpkins everywhere—both on the steps and the floor and also, thanks to her art skills with old, about-to-be-tossed-from-the-library-system books, paper ones sprouting from the pages of said books, hung upside down from the exposed rafters.

Thick layers of spray cobwebs adorned the front door and the windows as did chains of paper cranes they'd folded together in front of the TV last night while they'd watched *Jumanji*. A big, black, plastic cauldron sat on the welcome mat and, the piece-de-résistance, the jack-o'-lantern she and Jude had carved together this morning, sat glowing a warm, welcoming orange on top of the cauldron.

But the real magic had happened in the kitchen. Clem had bought the usual packaged, individually wrapped candy to give out to the trick or treaters but Jude was having none of it. He insisted on doing something unique and after buying an armload of good quality plain cooking chocolate from *Delish*—the new shop that had caused such a stir last year when it had been set up in direct competition to Sage's beloved Copper Mountain chocolate shop—he set about creating the most amazing individual chocolate treats.

Three dimensional trees made out of chocolate, their branches bare, with just a wisp of spray cobweb and a fondant spider or ghost hanging down. Little chocolate baskets for the individual wrapped candies. He'd even managed to fashion headless skeletons out of chocolate. It was Clem's job to wrap them in the clear cellophane bags he'd purchased and tie them off with ribbon but she'd stopped so often to admire his handiwork, she was way behind on the production line by the time Jude had finished.

"You'd have never made it in a Parisian kitchen," he said good-naturedly.

"I could have told you that before all this."

"You would have had your pay docked."

She blinked. "Really?"

"Hell, yes. Being an apprentice chef in Paris where every wannabe chef in the world wants to get their start? Restaurants know there are plenty of others willing to take your place if you don't work out, so you gotta work fast and fit in or you're gone."

"That sounds like an awful lot of pressure."

He shrugged. "It's not the way I like to run a kitchen but it does make you efficient." He glanced at the backlog of things to be wrapped and took a skeleton she'd just slipped into a bag out of her hands. "You bag 'em, I'll tie 'em."

"Yes, Chef," she mimicked and he groaned.

"Very funny."

"You don't like it?" she asked with faux innocence.

"I do not."

She'd been teasing but his voice had an edge to it. "You regret going on the show?"

"No." He shook his head. "It launched my career. Gave me a lot of opportunities, brought me a lot of accolades I wouldn't have had without it but…"

Clem waited for him to elaborate and prompted him when it appeared he wasn't going to finish his thought. "But?"

"I wasn't necessarily any better than any other chef on that show. With hindsight, I can see that it was a lot about timing and luck and a lot of benefiting from others screwing up. But that didn't stop my ego from exploding or walking around with a giant hard-on over myself thinking I was some kind of cooking wunderkind." He pulled the ribbon he'd been tying, tight, staring at his handiwork. "I don't think I liked that guy very much."

Trying not to get stuck on the *giant hard-on* bit and her acquaintance with it, Clem nudged his arm with her shoulder and said, "And what about this guy?"

He came out of his reverie to look down at her. "I don't know." He smiled. "What about this guy?"

His gaze seemed to burrow into hers and Clem's breath caught. What about him? He was just Jude to her—even when he'd been a distant celebrity. And right here, right now, standing side by side in her kitchen with the passage of time and one night of intimacy she hadn't been able to stop thinking about between them, he was still just Jude. Even if her feelings toward him were far more mature, far more nuanced now.

But that wasn't what he was asking and despite her instigating the question, Clem sought to lighten the mood. It was four thirty trick or treaters would be arriving soon and they needed to finish this so she could go slip into her costume. Not to mention they were entering murky waters.

"He's okay," she said flippantly.

Jude laughed. "Gee thanks. With friends like you I don't need enemies."

Friends—yes, right. Jesus, Clem... *friends*. Not whatever was causing the slight bump in her pulse.

And then he returned his attention to the bagging. "Tell me about the job in New York. You've barely mentioned it."

Clem grabbed the new conversational direction with both hands. "My friend, Sondra, the one I told you about at the Met?" He nodded and she continued. "She recommended me to this woman, Eliza Redgold, who's a private art collector who regularly buys and sells in the international market. She has several paintings coming to her in January with uncertain origins and she wants me to research their provenance."

"You know about art?" He whistled.

His forearm brushed against hers, as he reached for some more ribbon, skittering goose bumps all the way to Clem's shoulder. "Good lord, no. I've not got the first idea. But she's not hiring me for my artistic qualifications. She's hiring me for research capabilities. Provenance involves discovering the history of the ownership of a piece of art from the time it was produced until present day."

"And you know how to do that?"

She laughed at the streak of admiration in his voice. It felt good to be able to impress someone whose CV was pretty damn impressive, too. "No, not really but it's basically a research job so I'll figure it out. And Sondra will be a great resource."

"It sounds fascinating."

"I'm sure it would be."

"Would?"

"I called Elizabeth and pulled out of the job a couple of weeks ago."

Clem watched as his hands stilled and felt his eyes cut to her. "*What?* Why? January is still a couple of months away."

"I know. I just…" She shrugged as she continued to stuff skeletons into bags. "There's still so much unknown about the pace of Mom's recovery right now. If one thing my incessant research has taught me is that recovery is so very individual. If she continues on her current trajectory she'll be home and having day therapy before we know it. But it's too early to tell right now and I want to be there for her and Dad until things are more certain. That could be next month or six months away and I don't want to dick Eliza around in the meantime. I wanted to give her plenty of time to find a replacement."

It was the responsible thing to do. And Clem had always been responsible.

"Okay, that's admirable. But... it's not about the guilt thing, is it?"

Clem glanced up into his earnest expression, his brow furrowed in concern. "No." Well... maybe a little. But. "She's my mother, Jude. She's spent years of her life nurturing me. I'd be a pretty awful daughter if I got on with life when *she* needed a little nurturing. I know she has Dad and Marietta, but he needs support too and I'm capable *and* willing." She smiled at Jude who was still frowning. "I'm not turning my back on changing up my life. I just want to make sure they're going to be okay before I make my big move."

"Yeah, I get that," he conceded. "Just don't... lose sight of what you wanted, okay? Take it from me, life can get in the way and before you know it, ten years has gone by."

Clem heard regret echoed in his quiet, carefully chosen words and she would be lying if she wasn't a little worried about that happening. About life taking over and never putting her house on the market and going back to work at the library because the funds she'd so diligently set aside to tide her over until the new year were running low. About her ambitions going on the back burner out of guilt and duty.

And she appreciated him putting it out there.

"I'll do you a deal. Seeing as how you'll be sticking around, I give you permission to kick my butt into action if you see me stagnating again."

He smiled, his teeth nice and white amidst all the auburn-gingery goodness of his whiskers. The pale peridot of his eyes an unwavering calm. "You're on." He stuck his hand out. "As someone who has benefited gratefully from a Clementine Jones ass kicking, I would be proud to return the favor."

Clem laughed at the barely disguised glee in his voice. Now Jude was here and they'd reconnected, leaving Marietta would be even more of a wrench but knowing he had anointed himself keeper of her goals was strangely comforting. She slipped her hand into his, that now familiar awareness of him lighting her up everywhere. "Thank you," she murmured.

"What are friends for?" he teased.

And Clem's ribs suddenly felt way too tight for her lungs.

THE FIRST KNOCK on the door came at just after five and Clem hurried to answer it while straightening the back vertical seam of her silky black stockings. She'd gone for her usual witch outfit just a slightly less PG version most Marietta folk had come to expect from her.

But she wasn't the same Clem anymore, damn it, so why

not switch up the witch?

She ditched the grotesque mask complete with long black hair instead choosing a tiny black pointy hat pinned jauntily to her curls. Gone too were the thick white stockings with wide bands of black horizontal stripes and stilettos had replaced the pointy toed, hobnailed boots. Her eye makeup was subtle rather than horror-film dramatic—apart from the glossy red of her mouth—and her usual plain black dress was showing off some cleavage instead of being buttoned all the way up her neck.

Cleavage admirably assisted by the addition of a push-up bra.

"Jude," she called, looking over her shoulder one last time at the seams as she pulled up at the door. "They're here. Can you bring the treats?"

As she reached for the handle she heard a spooky, "*Bwa-ha-ha-ha,*" and glanced toward the kitchen to find Jude standing in the doorway, dressed as Dracula in head-to-toe black, including a cape with a collar that stood high and flashed red from the lining. His face was powdered, his lips were pulled back to expose fake pointy plastic teeth, his coppery hair gelled back into a prominent widow's peak.

He was the perfect comic book vampire. With red hair.

For some reason, Clem hadn't expected him to get in costume and she stared. He should look ridiculous—a grown man with a powdered face and gaudy plastic fangs—but hell if it didn't work for him. She'd never got the vampire attraction—this brand or the sparkly ones—but, good lord, she got it now.

He whistled bringing her out of her blatant ogling. "So,

what kind of a witch do you call that?" he asked as his gaze moved up and down her body. She hadn't dressed like this for Jude but her belly did a funny little dip at his scrutiny.

"Sexy witch." Shoving her hands on her hips, she stood tall in her spiky black heels. This was who she was now. Confident, go-getter, globe-trotting Clem. She straightened her shoulders. "Is it working?"

Okay... maybe she had dressed like this a teeny-tiny bit for Jude.

"Let's just say I think we might need some cardiac meds as well as the treats. For all the daddies and granddaddies."

His compliment made her a little dizzy but the second knock interrupted the buzz followed by little voices yelling, "Trick or treat."

Tamping down on the dizziness, Clem turned and opened the door to find three little moppets carrying orange pumpkin-shaped pails on the doormat. "Oh my goodness," Clem said pressing her hand to her chest. "It's Belle, Jasmine, and Mulan. Hey, Jude," she called over her shoulder, "how lucky are we?"

The little girls twirled around showing off their costumes then said, "Trick or treat," again in unison.

Jude swept in, brandishing his cape with a flourish and a well-timed, *"Bwah-ha-ha-ha,"* which had the little girls squealing in delight. They gasped in awe as he presented the bowl with all his carefully made goodies. "These are awesome," Mulan said, staring at her wrapped tree.

Clem nodded and pointed at Jude. "He made them."

All three girls gaped up at him. "You can cook?" Belle said, like it was the most miraculous thing she'd ever heard.

"He sure can," Clem confirmed. "He's the best."

"Wow," Jasmine said on a breath out as they continued to gaze at him like he was Santa Claus, the Easter bunny, the tooth fairy *and* a freaking unicorn all rolled into one.

He beamed down at them indulgently and she thought, *do not jump comic book vampire in front of kiddies.*

Instead she grabbed three origami cranes from the bowl on the hallstand and handed them over to three very impressed little customers who exclaimed their delight taking them with a thank you before heading down the path, skipping to a clutch of adults who hovered at the open gate.

Clem waved at the parents who all waved back as Jude said, "I think we win Halloween."

She laughed. "It's not a competition."

Snorting, he said, "Hell yes, it is. And we're going to win this one just as Marietta is going to win in the best-town category for the chocolate display competition."

Edwin had whipped himself into a frenzy organizing everything and Clem had read all about it in the local newspaper last week. An impartial judge from Helena—a local food critic—had been appointed and thanks to Facebook she knew shops from Bozeman to Livingstone and all the surrounding areas were busy planning how to decorate their windows once Halloween was over and they had their window spaces back.

Jude's displays at the Graff gift shop, which changed every few days, were popular around town but he'd hinted at something *very* grand for the week of the Marietta Stroll, which was when judging would take place.

"Still competitive, I see?"

He smiled. "Can't let Edwin down."

Clem was about to laugh but she heard the gate open and turned to greet their next customers, the six-year-old Roberts twins, making their way up the path in puppy dog costumes. "Wowsers, Clem," Calvin Roberts said from the gate as he clutched his chest dramatically, "you can put a spell on me any time."

She laughed. Calvin had gone to grade school with her and was married to one of her good friends—who was standing right beside him. Tina whacked him in the chest playfully. "Ignore him."

Jude leaned in and murmured, "Told you."

His breath licked inside her ear canal as deftly as if it had been his tongue and feathered down her neck into the exposed *V* of her cleavage. Her nipples tightened and Clem definitely wanted to shut the door and do him.

This burgeoning sexual attraction to her *friend* was rather inconvenient.

But then Jax and Dax were on the porch saying, "Trick or treat," and Jude was doing his *bwah-ha-ha-ha* thing and she thanked god for something else to do…

THREE HOURS LATER, the last trick or treaters were gone. They were out of paper cranes and candy and Clem was sitting cross-legged on the couch in her pajamas devouring Jude's gourmet mac and cheese and sipping on red wine as it snowed outside. He was in his pajamas—long flannel pants and a soft, well-worn T-shirt—doing the same.

It was warm and cozy as she stared at the fire dancing in the grate. If only she couldn't still feel the bubble of arousal from earlier simmering in her belly. Persisting despite him de-vamping and the vicious ache in her arches from her stilettos.

"Shall we put the movie on?" he asked as he scraped the last morsel of cheese sauce from his bowl.

They'd made plans to watch *Beetlejuice* tonight but maybe it would be wiser to retire to her room? Despite it not being quite eight thirty. That was far preferable to the ridiculous urge to drink red wine from Jude Barlow's navel.

But, if she went to bed now she'd just lay awake worrying about her mom. Clem didn't know how long it would be before she'd stop worrying about the potential of another stroke but it sure as hell wasn't yet.

"Sure."

He chuckled. "You don't sound very enthusiastic."

"Sorry." She shot him a self-deprecating smile. "I just haven't watched this much TV since my Buffy addiction."

He reached for Clem's empty bowl and leaned forward at the hips to deposit both on the coffee table. "You don't usually watch TV?"

"No." She shook her head. "I normally read at nighttime."

"Ah." He ran a hand over his jaw and the deliciously scratchy noise of his whiskers added to the simmer. "That explains why you have so many books."

Clem reached for the pad of origami paper on the coffee table and tore off a page. She needed to do *something* with hands itching to feel the prickle of those bristles. "You noticed," she said as she made her first fold.

"I did." He held out his hand for the pad and she handed it over. "There doesn't seem to be much fiction though?"

She shrugged as she kept her eyes on the paper. "I love novels but I like to keep on top of all the nonfic so I know what exactly to recommend, if possible, to students or customers looking for specific things. Plus so many of them are *fascinating*. I learn so much and I get totally lost in them. I love it when that happens, when you go to a different world and then you look up because you're thirsty or your ass has gone numb and two hours has passed and it feels like two minutes."

He laughed as his fingers also folded. "Yeah, I get that. I feel the same way about cooking. How absorbing it is to create the perfect dish or blending different tastes and textures to get that perfect *bite*. It's... exciting."

"Yes." Clem nodded enthusiastically, glancing at him then wishing she hadn't as the sight of his teeth pressing into his bottom lip in concentration gave her an alternative image for the *perfect bite*.

Returning her attention to her crane, she said, "There's nothing quite like that new book smell. Opening it for the first time and sniffing it, inhaling that amazing aroma of ink on the paper." She sighed. "It's like every birthday and Christmas morning memory for me all rolled into one. It's the smell of home and family and... love."

He lifted his head. "Yeah. Same. Food is love."

Their eyes met and held, their fingers stilling, and neither of them moved for what felt like an age. It was probably only a few seconds but in those heartbeats of time echoing loudly through her ears, Clem was sure she saw a streak of hunger in that startling peridot gaze. The same streak she knew must be lurking in her own amber one.

He *wanted* her, too, she was sure of it. *Holy mama.*

Then he blinked, dragging his attention from her face and reaching for the remote control. "Movie?" he asked, his voice decidedly strained.

"Yup," she agreed readily.

Anything. Anything to distract her from the hunger.

Chapter Eight

A COUPLE OF weeks later, Clem met up with Rhonda at the Graff. They'd had a cocktail at the bar then gone to the restaurant for something to eat. It was nice to catch up with her bestie again, considering Clem had turned into a bit of a recluse since her mother's stroke. She was at the hospital every afternoon and usually too exhausted—*mentally* exhausted—to do anything other than sit in front of the television at night folding paper cranes with Jude as they worked their way through an array of movies and she ignored the low-level sizzle buzzing between them.

Clem had taken the afternoon shift with her mom to make it easier on her dad who found the worsening roller coaster of Trina's emotions as each day progressed distressing. Especially as it was looking increasingly *un*likely that her mom would be home in time for Thanksgiving. Her recovery was slow despite her mother's determination and her optimism was flagging by the day.

Keeping Trina positive and motivated was a challenge and emotionally draining and Clem was grateful every day to have the side research project she was working on for Jude. Getting herself lost in a world of research—*food* research at that—was no hardship and the process proved to be absorbing as always. She already had a stack of articles and recipes printed and color-coded in her usual manner. Not to mention lists of references requiring further investigation.

And it was just *so* fascinating, immersing herself in the Great Plains and how the people who had inhabited the land both before and after the arrival of Europeans had fed themselves. She was unearthing some truly interesting information about both First Nations and colonial dining habits and she was absolutely *loving* it.

A large part of why the job in New York had appealed so much was the opportunity to research areas with which she was unfamiliar. Also, it felt *significant* to be doing something targeted. Being a librarian in a small town required her to be a jack-of-all-trades, which was fine but not earth-moving. To be able to pursue *one* thing in depth felt *important* as well as appealing to the academic side of Clem that had, she realized, languished over the years.

Jude's research was giving her a little taste of her future and had only reinforced how right the decision had been to shake up her life.

Clem spent a lot of the meal debriefing about her mom and the road ahead, which allowed her to avoid the topic she was pretty sure Rhonda wanted most to talk about—Jude. And then their chocolate brownies arrived decorated with jagged shards of maraschino cherry and rose white chocolate bark.

"Oh my," Clem said as she crunched into a corner which broke off with a satisfying snap. Her eyes closed as the sweet and tart melted on her tongue. "So good."

"Yeah, that Jude's sure a magician with chocolate."

When she opened her eyes, Rhonda was waiting, her shrewd gaze laser sharp. "How *are* things going with Jude?"

The question seemed innocent enough but she knew Rhonda. Her friend was capable of ninja levels of interrogation and Clem wished they could go back to discussing pureed meals and toileting issues.

Clem took a steadying breath. "Fine." But Rhonda just sat and waited for her to elaborate. "He's been so handy during this whole thing," she added, her nerves getting the better of her. "I don't think I've ever been fed better."

"So... he hasn't tried to propose again?"

She laughed. "Of course not. That was just... jet lag."

"Last time I had jet lag I obsessively cleaned the house at four in the morning for three nights in a row before I finally slept for two solid days. Didn't propose to a single person."

"It was a little... left of center," Clem admitted.

"I'll say. What if you'd said yes?"

"But I didn't." Picking up her spoon, Clem feigned interest in her brownie.

Rhonda did *not* pick up her spoon. In fact, she folded her arms. "There's no... weirdness, about it?"

Clem wasn't going to tell Rhonda that the proposal weirdness had been trumped by their one-night stand. She'd be like a dog with a bone in possession of that information. "Nope. Its fine," she dismissed. "We're just friends. He knows that. So do I."

Their *sizzle* didn't count.

"And might there be a situation where you could be more than friends? You are living together after all."

Clem glanced up from her brownie, startled. "We're not

living together."

Rhonda's raised eyebrows called bullshit. "What would you call it then?"

"He's a… house guest. He's staying with me until he can find a rental."

"He being Jude Barlow, ex-celebrity chef and all-round hottie?"

"We're *friends*. And even if we weren't, I have enough on my plate right now, don't you think?"

Those eyebrows drew together. Rhonda had never understood holding back—in anything. Where Clem was measured, her bestie was impulsive. "You have to acknowledge he is a hottie, right?"

Good lord, Rhonda had *no* idea. A hottie with *skills*. "Yes."

"So… ever heard of friends with benefits? I know Clem 2.0 is open to a holiday fling, why not a Marietta fling?"

"Because we're—"

"Friends," Rhonda finished.

"Yes." She frowned at her bestie. "And when I leave next year, and he stays and the *fling* is over, how do we get back to what we had before?" They'd managed one night okay but a fling was a whole other kettle of fish.

"You and Reuben seem to manage okay."

"Reuben and I weren't—"

"Yes, you were," Rhonda interrupted. "You were friends before you started dating."

"We were *friendly*, not friends." And they'd fallen into a mutually convenient sexual relationship but it had never been anything too serious. Sure, the sex had been good and it had been nice to have a plus-one to accompany her places but they were much better friends—now—than they'd ever been as partners. "Not like what Jude and I had. *Have*."

There was too much history in their friendship to survive a romance gone wrong.

"Now…" Clem continued, "if Jude had just been passing through for a few days or a couple of weeks and then gone again… maybe a dalliance could have worked." She took a beat to let the delicious possibilities of *that* sink into her brain. "But he's making Marietta his home and I'm on my way out. We both have things we want to achieve. It would be stupid to derail that now we've *finally* figured those things out."

"It could be even stupider to not let it play out."

"Until it came to the end and we wrecked a perfectly good friendship."

"What if"—Rhonda leaned in on her elbows in a conspiratorial fashion—"it didn't have to end? There are these things called planes and you know, *the internet*. There's even," she lowered her voice, "*phone sex*. New York's not that far away, Clem, and long-distance relationships *can* work."

Clem refused to give the lure of such thoughts any oxygen. She couldn't start anew, move forward, while looking back. If she was serious about switching up her life she had to embrace what was in the future and give it a fair shot—not be pining over something she'd left behind. Right?

"What I really need is him to be a friend right now. And I need *you* to drop it."

"Okay, okay." Rhonda threw her hands up in surrender as she flopped back into her chair. "Fine." She picked up her spoon then casually asked, "Do you mind if I have a crack then?"

Clem blinked, *stunned*, at the question. She shouldn't mind—Rhonda was a great person who she loved dearly. And, objectively speaking, she and Jude would probably make a great couple. But, yeah, she minded.

She *seriously freaking minded*.

"Oh my god." Rhonda burst out laughing. "You should see your face right now." She shook her head. "Friend my ass."

Then she grinned and stabbed her fork into the brownie.

JUDE HEARD THE door open at eight thirty and called, "In the kitchen."

Clementine appeared in the doorway moments later looking tired but relaxed in dark blue jeans and a hot pink sweater that was all fuzzy and fluffy with a row of very distracting little pearly white buttons down the front.

He was thankful he hadn't seen her before she'd gone for dinner. He'd have thought about nothing else other than how much he wanted to pop them open and strip her out of it…

Which was why the phone call he'd received earlier was a good thing.

"How was your meal?" he asked, returning his attention to what he was doing and *not* the sweater.

She sighed. "Lovely. I'm stuffed full."

"You had dessert?"

"Of *course*." The *duh* in her voice made him smile. "I had the brownie and your bark looked and *tasted* awesome."

"Thanks." He glanced up, keeping his eyes trained on her face. "I was happy with how it turned out."

"And everyone was talking about your Cinderella carriage display across the foyer."

He grinned. "I was *really* pleased with how that turned out."

It had been his most elaborate so far as he warmed up his artistic skills for the grand extravaganza in three weeks. Yesterday, he'd met with Sage from Copper Mountain Chocolates and Viv from *Delish* and they'd been strategizing their windows, bouncing ideas off each other so Marietta could put its best foot forward in the competition.

"Did you see the latest notes I left for you?" She tipped her chin toward the orange plastic document folder she'd placed on the counter under the microwave overhang before she'd left for the hospital earlier.

"I did, thank you. I'm definitely going to be doing something with that bison pot roast recipe."

"I thought that might appeal to the carnivore in you," she said with a smile as she pushed off the doorway. "What are you doing there?"

Jude dropped his gaze to the multiple dots of chocolate on cooking paper as she drew closer. "Edwin was approached by a guy who wants to propose to his girlfriend on Friday night. The thing is, she's severely visually impaired and he asked if we could somehow create a chocolate dessert in braille that spells out will you marry me."

"Oh," she said breathily as she pulled up beside him.

"That is so cool."

"It is." The fuzz from her sweater brushed his arm and Jude realized how close they were standing, their hips almost pressing together.

"Is that the phrase there?" she asked, pointing at a piece of paper near his elbow.

"Yep. That's, *will you marry me* in braille. And now I just have to work out what's the best medium and chocolate consistency and required proportions to deliver the message with accuracy. There are braille molds you can buy but hand scripting is so much more personal, don't you think?"

"Yes. Absolutely."

Jude made the fatal mistake of glancing at her as she glanced at him, smiling a smile that was full of admiration and her fuzzy arm was brushing his and he fought the urge to drop his head and place a kiss on those upturned lips. God knew he *wanted* to.

More than that it felt like the most natural thing to do standing here in her kitchen, side by side. He returned her smile.

"I suppose you've had a few proposal requests over the years like this?"

Dragging his eyes off her, Jude went back to squeezing warm chocolate from the piping bag. "Oh god, yes."

"What's the most memorable?"

Her gaze was hot on his knuckles as she followed his movements and Jude gripped the bag a little firmer as he continued his piping.

"A few months after *Hey Jude* opened, a guy asked us to bake one of our signature fortune cookies and slip the ring inside after which we managed just fine. The cookie was put on the plate and brought out at the end of the meal as arranged. The fortune strip had will you marry me on it and it was sitting on the plate, not inside the cookie. The plan was that she'd read the strip and he'd tell her to crack the cookie."

"Oh dear," she murmured. "This isn't going to end well is it?"

Jude smiled as he piped. "It did not. Before he could say anything there was a bit of a commotion at the front of the restaurant which grabbed everyone's attention and while everyone was gawking at it, she popped the cookie in her mouth and crunched into it."

Gasping, Clementine said, "What happened?"

Jude grinned. "She broke her tooth and had to have emergency dental work done. She was furious with him."

"Oh no." Clementine clapped her hand over her mouth. "That poor woman."

He laughed. "I know."

"Don't laugh." She nudged her elbow into his side. "It's awful." But then she laughed, too.

"After that we brought in veto rights over all food related proposals."

"*Did* they get married?"

"Apparently, yes."

Clementine shook her head. "God... what if she'd swallowed it? Or choked on it."

"Honestly? I think she'd have preferred that to breaking her tooth."

And they laughed again. When it settled, Clementine

glanced at the rows of chocolate dots of varying sizes and configurations. "Who's going to eat all these dots?"

"Not you."

"Hey," she pouted up at him, her eyebrows beetling. "Why not?"

"I thought you were stuffed full?" he teased.

"Jude," she tsked him then, a big smile on her face. "There is always room for chocolate. And they're just dots." She lifted off one of the larger dots and balanced it on her index finger. "They'll melt on the tongue before they even make it to my stomach."

Popping it into her mouth, Clementine shut her eyes on a sigh, her mouth moving as she obviously savored the treat and Jude wondered how she tasted right now, her tongue coated in chocolate. Sweet for sure. Addictive—definitely.

Crap... this attraction was becoming harder and harder to manage.

Then her eyelids fluttered open and their gazes locked and they stared at each other for long drawn-out moments. Her tongue flicked out to swipe along her bottom lip either from nervousness or the presence of chocolate and Jude had to bite back a groan, suppress the urge to take her mouth, sample the sweet delights of that bottom lip.

See for himself. *Taste* for himself.

Blood pounded through his veins, pulsing hot to his wrists and temples and abdomen, throbbing hard in his groin. And if she'd been any other woman, he'd have swooped in. But it wasn't. It was Clementine. And he was Jude.

And *they* were complicated.

Clamping down hard on a body going rogue, he forced a smile to his mouth and threw some mental cold water on the moment. Drawing away a little to put as much space as possible between them considering the proximity of their hips, he said, "I got a phone call from the Realtor today."

"Has he found you the perfect inn?"

Jude chuckled. "No. But there's a two-bedroom rental over near the hospital that'll become available second week in December."

"Oh." A tiny little *V* formed between her brows. "Well, that's… great."

She smiled but it looked forced and it didn't sound like she thought it was great. Whatever that meant?

"Finally, your own place, right?"

"Yeah. I'll be out of your hair in a few weeks."

Shrugging, she said, "I liked having you in my hair." She blinked. "I mean…" Giving a tremulous half-laugh, she shook her head. "That didn't sound right."

Jude grinned. "It's okay, I know what you meant. For what it's worth I liked being in your hair, too."

Even given his inconvenient attraction, he wouldn't have traded his time in Clementine's house. He'd enjoyed it too damn much. Enjoyed how their friendship had deepened to something more mature, more evolved from their childhood connection. The companionship of nights together, time in the kitchen together, eating together, watching TV together.

The paper cranes.

He'd never just sat still and *been* with a woman. His celebrity had altered *all* his relationships, with the opposite sex in particular, and he'd worn himself out being the guy he'd figured women wanted in a celebrity.

Flashy dates, A-list parties, being seen at all the right places.

It had been exhausting. And he'd kidded himself into thinking he was happy because he'd *made it.* So many wannabes and *he'd* made it. When the truth was he'd never been happier than when he'd helped Clementine decorate her porch and dish out Halloween treats to excited little kiddies in a black cape and plastic fangs. He'd never felt as right about anything as he'd done when he'd talked to the Marietta Relator about finding himself an inn.

A decade ago, his dream to own a country inn had seemed too *small* in the spotlight of his sudden fame. Now, it was the perfect fit.

"You know what this means?" she said, her voice brisk as she took a little step to the side, increasing the space between them and crossing her arms.

It took every ounce of willpower Jude owned not to check out how much tighter her sweater had pulled. He returned to his piping. "No, what?"

"We're going to need to get folding."

After Halloween, they'd set a target of folding a thousand origami cranes together. The Japanese tradition that a thousand paper cranes could make one special wish come true had appealed to Clementine's goal-orientated soul and his competitive nature.

It also gave them something else to do with their hands.

"We'll surely be done by then? But even if we're not, there's no reason why we can't still get together for a friendly origami sesh after I leave."

Except for these feelings he wasn't entirely sure were *friendly* anymore.

"True. But let's see if we can't smash it out before that."

"Sure," he said, concentrating hard on the piping nozzle. "Fine by me."

"You still up for *The Martian* tonight?"

"Yep, another fifteen or so?"

"Cool." She pushed away from the counter and Jude felt both relief and loss. "I'll get changed and be reading in the living room whenever you're ready."

She walked away then and Jude resisted looking up for one second, two seconds, three. And then he succumbed, catching a brief glimpse of that pink sweater as she disappeared from sight.

But not, unfortunately, from mind.

CLEM COULDN'T BELIEVE how fast two weeks had flown by as she got home from the hospital the day before Thanksgiving. She normally got in between five and six but her watch said four thirty as she let herself into her house. Her father, who usually arrived at the hospital about five had turned up at four, as planned, so Clem could double-check on the arrangements for her mom tomorrow.

Trina's medical team hadn't been ready to discharge her home yet, which had been a huge blow for her mom but, they had suggested a day pass for tomorrow, which she'd grabbed with both hands. This year, more than any other, they had much to be thankful for and getting to be together at *home* as a family, even for a reduced time, was precious.

So, while her father and Jude, who was staying in Marietta for Thanksgiving—his mom was on a cruise and his father was at some crane symposium in Canada—had taken care of the meal planning, Clem had tasked herself with the logistics of transport and equipment that would be required. And, satisfied that everything was organized and ready to go for the morning, she'd headed home.

The warmth of the house was wonderful compared to the biting chill outside and Clem's nostrils flared at the aroma's wafting from the kitchen. Pumpkin spice and cloves. She'd miss this—her house smelling like a Michelin star restaurant—when Jude left. Hell, who was she kidding? She'd miss Jude, period.

It was necessary, she knew. Sensible. *Of course*, he needed the permanency of his own place. But Clem couldn't deny the tiny tug in her chest at the thought of him moving out.

She discarded her jacket, laptop, and bag in her room before wandering to the kitchen. Pulling up short in the doorway she blinked at a *shirtless* Jude. Every atom of saliva in her mouth evaporated as her eyes were drawn to the broad outline of his shoulders, the definition of his pecs and the firm pillowed plank of his abs.

A smattering of red-gold hair around his nipples was equally fascinating but not as fascinating as the trail that trekked downward form his navel.

Down. Down. Down.

An image of her following that line southward with her tongue had her salivary glands performing a rapid reverse action, her mouth flooding with moisture. And somewhere, a lone frantic brain cell ordered her to *stop looking*. Just *stop*.

But she *wasn't* listening.

Thankfully, he hadn't seen her yet. His ear pods were jammed firmly in place and his head bopped to what she assumed was music as he bent over the central counter, piping bag in hand.

Frankly she didn't want to make any sudden movements in case he did see her.

Somewhere, no doubt, there was a hell for her, but right now, she was just fine at the prospect of dancing with the devil. Of course, he chose that moment to look up and bust her staring at him with her mouth open like a sideshow alley clown.

"Oh damn, sorry." He popped his ear pods out. "I wasn't expecting you home yet."

Clem forced her mouth shut with a click. "Dad got to the hospital a bit earlier today." She tipped her chin at his chest as nonchalantly as she could considering the mere sight of it made her a little breathless. "Did I interrupt some alone time?"

He laughed. "Sorry, no. I knocked a pint of milk with my elbow. I made a dive for it to save it from crashing to the ground but my shirt copped most of it." He glanced at the sodden mess of a discarded T-shirt at the end of the counter as he put down the piping bag. "I'll go grab another."

Clem flapped his suggestion away with her hand. "It's fine." His chest wasn't exactly hard to look at. It was certainly spilt milk she *wouldn't* be crying over. "Not anything I haven't seen before."

Oh, Jesus… why had she said *that*? But it was out there

between them now and it was clear from his raised eyebrow and the small smile on his mouth that he was thinking about the night they'd had sex.

"I think the first time I ever met you, you were sans shirt," she said because normalizing this situation seemed imperative right now.

"It was summer. I was *eight*."

Yeah, it had been and he was. And there was *zero* comparison between that scrawny, rib-rutted version and the hard magnificence of this mature one.

Desperate to change the subject, Clem pushed off the doorframe and wandered into the kitchen. "What's cooking?"

"Pies for tomorrow," he murmured, as he returned his attention to what he was doing.

Clem's mouth watered at the thought as she moved to his left. Pushing his ear pods out the way, she boosted herself up onto the countertop of the central island aided by the slide of her long, flowy black velvet skirt. She was about a foot away from his hip and a bunch of trays, piping bags and bowls of varying sizes some of which contained what appeared to be chocolate mousse.

Maybe being this close to all that naked male flesh was a mistake but Clem was determined to act like it was no big deal. And that she'd totally moved on from their one night together.

"Are these also for tomorrow?" she asked as he piped the mousse into small chocolate cups. Ones he'd, no doubt, made himself.

"Yep." He put down the bag and switched to another.

There were four in total all about a quarter full.

"I didn't realize chocolate mousse was on the menu?"

"It's not, officially. But I want to do these for the Graff stall at the stroll, so this is my practice batch. I'm experimenting with different flavors to see what works best to give them a little extra kick."

Each cup was filled quickly and efficiently as he spoke with what was obviously a much-practiced rotation of his wrist. The end result was uniform swirls rising to a perfect peak.

"You look like you've done that before," she murmured.

"Once or twice. You want a go? I can teach you if you like? Learn from a professional and all that."

He glanced up at her, grinning, and Clem gave a half-laugh. But she could see no purpose in interrupting perfection for the mediocre. "I'm much more interested in helping *you* decide on the flavors. Learn from the professional and all that," she mimicked.

He straightened and she high-fived herself on keeping her eyes *up* and not *down* where the broad sweep of his firm, pale pecs met the puckered perfection of his abs. "Professional, huh?"

Clem held up her hand, her middle three fingers raised like she was about to take a Girl Scout pledge. "Card carrying chocolate mousse aficionado."

"Aficionado? Hmm… all right then." He put the piping bag down. "Tell me what these flavors are."

Opening the nearby top drawer, he grabbed several teaspoons and dipped the first one into a bowl, scooping up some mousse and handing it over. Without hesitation, Clem slipped it into her mouth. The cold airy sweetness burst like candy canes on her tastebuds.

"Easy," she scoffed, her feet absently swinging back and forth as she savored the taste. "Mint."

He grinned and dipped another spoon into the next bowl. "And this one?"

Clem took the spoon and repeated the process as she toed off her winter boots. They *clunked* to the ground one by one and she wished she could peel off her thick woolen knee-highs, too. It was hot in here with the central heating and the oven.

And a half-naked Jude...

Her pink fluffy sweater didn't help. It might have been one of her favorites and perfect for going out on a cold winter's night but a little too hot for inside. "Mmm, that tastes like..." She concentrated on the earthy yet sweet tang of the mousse. "Mulled wine?" she murmured, as she pushed the sweater sleeves up to her elbows one at a time.

"Not bad," he admitted grudgingly. "It's clove, cardamom, and cinnamon so that's close enough."

"I think the word you're after is aficionado."

"Hmm." He narrowed his eyes at her. "Cocky, aren't you?"

She shrugged even as her breath hitched over his choice of word. It wasn't anything sexual, she knew, but the man *was* half naked, could she help it if her brain went there?

"Okay, little Miss Food Taster, try this one."

Another spoon was passed across and Clem eagerly consumed it. The flavor was subtle to begin with—but then it grew warmer on her tongue and she knew. "Mmm." She shut her eyes, pressing her lips together and savoring the delicious kick. When she opened them again his gaze was travelling up and down the row of buttons on her sweater.

And things got *hotter*.

"Chili," she murmured, her breath turning husky. "I like it."

He dragged his gaze up to her face. "Not too… intense?"

Clem shook her head. Not the chili anyway. "I mean… I'd label it for those who aren't fans of hot and spicy but…"

"Who even are those people?" he asked, a frown drawing his brows together.

"I know, right?"

Their gazes held for a beat or two and their combined puzzlement over non-chili people took a turn for the *even hotter* for long suspended moments.

One second, two seconds, three.

She could hear her heart in her ears, feel it fluttering at her temples and beat between her legs. Her breath had turned to sand in her lungs. But then his mouth slowly creased into a smile and hers followed suit and then they were grinning at each other and the ledge they'd been standing on pushed back out of reach.

"Okay." He cleared his throat and turned his attention to a fourth spoon. "I bet you can't get this one."

She relieved him of the utensil. "Challenge accepted." The sharp tang of citrus flooded her tongue and she had to stop herself from moaning out loud—neither of them needed any more provocation. "Really?" She rolled her eyes at him. "That's citrus."

He shook his head. "No, no. That's way too general. You

know how much citrus there is out there? More information please."

"Fine." Clem huffed out a breath in mock exasperation, her legs swinging gently. "Let me try some more."

Grinning, he handed her an actual chocolate cup this time and the same spoon. Clem dipped in again, loading it up for full effect. Shutting her eyes, she concentrated on the flavors as they sparked across her tongue and *not* the intensity of his presence.

"It's orange," she declared when she finally opened her eyes. It wasn't tart enough for lemon or lime.

Crossing his arms, he slowly shook his head. "Nope."

Hmm, okay, the man was playing hard ball. "*Blood* orange?"

He chuckled and it was as smooth and light as his chocolate mousse. "Nope."

Taking another spoonful, she tried again. Tipping her head back, her eyelids fluttered closed again because all that bare skin of his was far too distracting. Who could think when it was this hot? Her brain was practically cooking. "It's too sweet for grapefruit. Unless…" She glanced at him and his eyes drifted up from her buttons to meet hers. "Ruby grapefruit is sweeter, right?"

"Right."

"Right?" Clem brightened. "I'm right? It's a ruby grapefruit?"

"No." He grinned. "You're right about ruby grapefruits being sweeter."

Exasperated, she took another spoonful trying to guess while cataloging the fruit she knew was around Marietta this time of year. "I give in."

"What?" He uncrossed his arms and pressed a hand to his chest feigning shock. "Don't tell me the aficionado has been stumped?"

"Yeah, yeah, enough with the dramatics." And the drawing of attention to his chest and how close his fingertips were to his left nipple. "Spill."

He bugged his eyes at her. "It's a clementine."

She blinked. "What?" Clem had tasted the fruit once as a kid when she'd been on a school trip to California. "Since when do we get clementines around here?"

"Edwin got them in for me."

Well, that was interesting information. "You requested clementines?"

His hand dropped from his chest. "How could I not?"

He was teasing. She knew that. But it made her heart do a funny little wobble behind her ribs anyway.

"Well then." She smiled at him. "It's definitely my favorite."

"Mine, too."

Their gazes met and they were smiling at each other again but there was an undercurrent that was hard to ignore. Clem was determined to give it her best shot, though.

Digging her spoon into the mousse again, she said, "These cups are cute. You like making these kinds of things, yeah?"

"Sure." He shrugged. "They're not that hard once you know how and they're attention grabbing. You can make them as elaborate as you want and eating chocolate off chocolate is kinda decadent, don't you think?"

Clem didn't say anything, too busy thinking about how *decadent* it would be to eat chocolate off his *body*. Lick it off those smooth pecs. That ridge that bisected his abdomen. And those flat, male nipples. Also parts a little… lower.

"You don't agree?"

"Hmm?" She focused back in on his question. "Oh, sure. Yeah…"

One thick, dark male eyebrow raised in challenge. "But?"

"I was just…"

Clem breathed out an unsteady breath as a slew of erotic images rather unhelpfully scrolled like a movie reel through her dirty, dirty mind. She glanced down at the half cup of mousse still in her possession. Was clementine some kind of… aphrodisiac? Because her body was melting down with possibilities, her pulse a low, slow thump, flushing through neglected erogenous zones.

And if he'd let it drop, she could have pulled herself back from the temptations running wild through her head and thudding through her veins. *But he didn't.*

"Just?" he prompted. And it was low and slow too, keeping tempo with the pulse of her body.

"I was just thinking." Her voice sounded like fine-grade sandpaper as she dropped her eyes to her mousse. "About other things you could eat chocolate off."

Clem was close enough and at just the right level, to catch the thick bob of his whiskery throat as her gaze rose again. Their eyes met and she could see desire warring with caution in those pale green depths. Her breath held as the battle played out and Clem hoped like hell it was desire because even though she knew she shouldn't want him like this—that they were on two different paths right now—god help her, she *did*.

He cleared his throat. "Like what?"

Chapter Nine

A COOL STREAK of relief blasted through the heat at Clem's center. Whether it was wise or not she didn't really care right now. Nor, apparently did he, as his gaze zeroed in on her mouth like he wanted to smear it in mousse and lick up every last, sticky trace.

Her pulse tripped as she dipped her index finger into the cold, sweet fluff. She was so damn aroused at the sensation and the passion burning in his eyes her nipples tightened. Scooping up a portion she raised it to her mouth, his eyes tracking the movement with fevered intensity. Neither of them said anything as she pressed it to her lips but, Jude's breathing roughened as her lips closed around her finger.

Clem let it linger inside, hyperaware of him watching her, of his dilated pupils as her cheeks hollowed and her tongue swirled until it was all gone. Slowly her finger slid out with a wet kind of *phfft* that had Jude's nostrils flaring.

White, hot wanton need speared her to the counter.

"Yeah…" he murmured after a loaded moment. "That's pretty decadent."

"Uh-huh," Clem agreed, huskily. And she was hungry for more. Hell, she was *ravenous*. "The possibilities are endless."

She wriggled across the one foot that separated them, her slippery skirt easing the way until her thigh was pressing into his hip. If she'd wanted, she could have leaned in and dropped a kiss on top of the big, rounded haunch of his shoulder. Instead, she dipped her finger into her cup again, scooping up a dollop and lifting it to his mouth.

"Your turn."

Clem's breath hitched when his lips parted and he leaned in to suck her finger into the hot, wet cavern of his mouth. A ragged sigh slid from her lips and her pulse trebled at the electric swirl of his tongue. He might as well be licking between her legs now because that was exactly where she was feeling it as he held her gaze and sucked her finger clean.

She whimpered, a sound that came from the deep, dark recesses of her throat but also from someplace that wasn't *of* her body.

A place utterly primal.

Clearly satisfied that he'd done a proper job, he relinquished her finger, pulling away very, *very* slowly. Her finger made the same wet *phht* as it slid from Jude's mouth and she almost moaned at the loss of the heat and the wet and the *sex* of it.

Dropping her gaze, she contemplated his chest. The defined ridge of his collarbone looked like a good place, as did the hollow at the base of his throat. But his nipples called to her like a siren song and, watching herself as if she was out of her body, she smeared the mousse onto the pinky-brown surface. The quick, sharp intake of his breath and the way his nipple hardened beneath the pad of her finger had Clem salivating.

She didn't wait—she couldn't. No time to admire how good he looked or contemplate how he might taste. When her finger was done, her mouth followed and she swore she could feel the deep low rumble of his groan vibrating against her lips as they closed over his nipple and *sucked*.

He definitely swayed as she licked at the mousse, uncovering the sweet treat beneath and his hand slid just north of her knee and *gripped*. Her thigh buzzed, little bolts of electricity shooting up the inside, touching down right between her legs, zapping at her clitoris.

Clem was dizzy when she was finally satisfied with the job she'd done and lifted her head. Her belly looped twice at the ragged pant of his breath and the way his pupils all but obliterated the peridot of his eyes leaving only a thin rim of pale green.

"See?" she asked, her pulse thrumming through her ears. "Endless."

"Yeah." His voice sounded raw and he swallowed. "I see."

Then his hand slid to her other knee, applying pressure, urging her legs apart and boldly stepping between them when she opened. But he wasn't content with just standing there, his hand reaching for the fabric of her skirt and dragging it up—*up, up, up*—his gaze falling on her knees as they were bared, his hands traveling higher and higher on her exposed flesh until it was rucked high on her thighs.

Clem's pulse thrummed *everywhere* now, the heat between her legs flaring.

"Take here, for example," he murmured.

Lifting his gaze, he met and captured hers as he dipped a

finger in the nearest mousse. Clem didn't know the flavor, she didn't care, all she was conscious of was the pebbling of her nipples as the cool mousse met the hot flesh of her thigh and the intensity in his eyes. They held her in his thrall as he smeared the mousse in a line stopping just above her knee.

And when he dipped his head—lower and lower and lower—her breath hitched until the first warm puff of air caressed her skin and she let it out on a rush, more moan than sigh, and she thanked god she'd worn a skirt today.

The sear of his tongue had her reaching involuntarily for his head, her hand pushing into the short length of his chestnut hair and holding tight. This was how it would look Clem thought absently.

When he went down.

His reddy-brown head between her legs, his breath hot on her thighs. Her knuckles turning white as she held him firmer, urging him to keep going without saying a word. But then he stopped and his head lifted as his hands slid to the sides of her thighs, his tongue darting out to lap at first his bottom lip, then his top, which turned everything inside her belly to jelly.

"That was a… good example," Clem said, as his gaze dropped and settled on the buttons of her sweater.

"Oh, I'm definitely getting the hang of it. This sweater." His eyes lifted. "Is it new? Or expensive?"

"Neither." Clem swallowed, her voice ridiculously husky as his eyes dropped again, staring at those buttons like he was trying to pop them through sheer will power alone. "It's a favorite though."

His jaw clenched and unclenched for a beat or two as if

he was weighing up his options. "Fuck it," he muttered. "I'll buy you another one."

Then his hands slid to the hem, grasping it on either side of the buttons, and ripping in an upward motion. Clem gasped as they popped and flew everywhere. Pinging off the counter. The fridge behind them. The floor.

She stared at where, mere seconds ago, her sweater had been but was now her bare belly, and her breasts encased in a green-and-blue, satin-and-lace demi cup bra. "I could have undone them."

"Not fast enough," he growled absently as he stared at her, too. Like he was trying to commit every inch of her to memory. Hell, he was staring so damn hard she wondered if he was trying to calculate the weight of each boob, his gaze utterly *intent*.

"Does this thing require a degree in aeronautical engineering to get it undone or should I just rip it as well?"

Clem laughed, a wild thrill shooting through her at his careless impatience. "It's a front clasp."

He broke into a smile that turned her belly over several times. "The *best* kind."

His hand slid onto her stomach sparking electricity and Clem shivered as his fingers trekked upward not pausing as they delved into her cleavage. It took a second to find the clasp during which time his knuckles brushed against the inner slopes of her breasts, hardening her nipples and spreading goose bumps in their wake. Then he had it, the cups falling away, freeing her fully to his gaze.

"Jesus," he whispered as he watched her breasts swing free. "You have the nicest fucking tits."

Nipples, already pebbled, turned to taut peaks beneath the hot rove of his gaze and the filthiness of his mouth. Clem knew the librarian stereotype that was out there in the public should have her not approving of such crude language. But she loved language of all types and she freaking *loved* that Jude was looking at her breasts like they were a five-course degustation dinner for one.

And she was *no* prudish librarian.

A fact she proved when a dollop of cold mousse landed on her heated nipple and she gasped then moaned, "*Fuuck.*" When his mouth followed, hot and urgent, licking at first then sucking, pulling on the engorged tip so damn *hard*, her words weren't even intelligible.

But for sure, had they been remotely translatable, they'd have been cuss words.

"God, I want to eat all of you," Jude whispered, his head lifting briefly to scoop up more mousse and smear it on the other nipple before following through again with his mouth, licking and sucking and swirling, devouring it, eating up every last bit.

It was so damn good Clem's neck ceased being able to support her head and she clutched at his nape as she lost the battle, her hair brushing her shoulder blades, her pulse crashing and her lungs heaving and little darts of pleasure traveling from her nipples to the hard, raised nub between her thighs, already pulsing in response. And when his hands spanned her ass and pulled her in tight against him, the roaring ache between her legs finding the roaring hardness between his, she actually thought she was going to come.

"Jude." She raised her head—with difficulty—as his fingers pinched and toyed with her nipples. Her pulse was like a water-hammer through her veins, her fingers shaking as she reached for his fly and yanked it down. "Condom," she panted and she didn't care how feral it sounded as her hand reached for his underwear.

She needed more. She needed all of him. She needed the hardness pressing between her legs pounding inside her.

"Wallet," he muttered around a nipple, not lifting his head, not relinquishing his mouthful. "Back pocket." And returned to what he was doing with a vengeance.

Abandoning her attempt to get into his underwear, Clem blindly groped for his pocket, her fingers finding the wallet and yanking it out. Raising it above his head, she opened it, finding the square foil and grabbing it, tossing the wallet who-knew-where, as she attempted to open the packet. It was no easy feat given she could barely see through the haze of lust caused by Jude's hot, wet mouth and her hands shaking so damn hard but, after several attempts, she got there.

A triumphant cry slipped from her mouth as she tossed the foil aside and reached between them again, yanking down his underwear, finding the steely hard length of him and wrapping her fingers around. He groaned, hot air rushing out around her nipple, the deep rumbly noise traveling straight through the wall of her chest.

"*Jesus Christ*," he swore as he finally released her from the torture of his tongue and Clem felt his blasphemy *everywhere*.

In her throat, in her gut, in her clitoris.

Pressing his forehead to the center of her chest, he grunted as her fingers found the taut crown of his cock. Hot air fanned her skin from his rough pants as Clem slipped the latex sheath down his girth.

"Now," she said urgently, her pulse a drumbeat surging through her temples, thrumming through her blood, throbbing between her legs. She angled him toward her with one hand, and swept her underwear aside with the other. "Please, Jude."

The need for Jude had become more and more frantic, rising like a marauding beast. It was so freaking bad that she'd get on her knees and beg him for it if she had to.

But she didn't have to.

He just lifted his head, his mouth taking hers, kissing her hot and hard, as he banded his arm around her back, slid a hand between them to notch himself at her entrance and, grabbing her hip, shoved into her *hard*.

Clem cried out, clutching at his shoulder as the thrust tore the breath from her lungs. Clearly the height of the countertop was just right for going *deep*.

"Oh god, sorry," he panted, breaking away, his eyes blazing as he looked down into hers, his forehead creased in concern. "Did I—"

"No." Clem shook her head vehemently, reveling in the hard ridge of him searing like a brand inside her. "It's good…" She breathed out unsteadily. "It's *really* good."

"Goddamn," he muttered. "So good."

"I want it just like this."

Then she slid her hand onto his nape and pulled him closer, meeting his lips halfway, wrapping her legs around his hips, keeping them locked tight as he groaned into her mouth, kissing her *hard*, too.

Kissing her like he was starving. Fucking her like they were dying.

And Clem reveled in it, her hips rising to meet his every thrust, their bodies practically sparking with each slam of his hips, the depth exquisite, the angle perfect, stoking and stoking, tossing her higher and higher chasing the orgasm that was rippling along her pelvic floor, starting to fray the line between heaven and earth.

Wanting it. Needing it. Needing *Jude* to give it to her. Only Jude. Jude who'd been back in her life for such a short time but had fast become *everything*.

Jude who was starting to tremble now—starting to grunt.

"Jude." Her voice was a low keen as the muscles that cocooned his every thrust started to tighten, started to clamp, the ripples turned hotter, growing stronger. "Oh god… Jude…"

"I know," he muttered, his mouth tearing from hers as he buried his forehead in her neck, leaning in to the angle, his hips snapping with each thrust, his shoulders shaking beneath her palms.

Her head jerked and her breasts jiggled and her orgasm broke.

In a sudden crash, it was upon her and Clem cried out with the force of it, clamping around him good and hard and tight as he gritted his teeth and pushed through, grunting with the effort of it until he *bellowed* and came, too, his movements jerking to a halt for one beat, two beats, three beats, clutching her close as he spilled inside her, their hearts beating as one, then resuming again, driving them through their release, driving them all the way to the end until they were done and were slumped in each other's arms, two panting wrecks.

He eased back a little when their breathing had returned to something more like normal but he didn't withdraw and Clem's breath stuttered out as the action emphasised just how hard he still was inside her. God, she must look utterly disheveled—her skirt hitched up, the tatters of her sweater hanging down around her elbows along with her bra, red marks on her chest from the scratch of his stubble, her nipples swollen from his attention.

If only there were any fucks to give in her post-orgasmic hum.

"So…" He smiled, his hand raising to brush at the curls on her forehead. "That happened again."

Clem returned his smile with a half one of her own. "Yeah."

"You want to talk about it?"

"I suppose we should." She bit into her bottom lip. Man, being an adult sucked sometimes.

But… the thing was, this time didn't feel as clear-cut as last time where a little bit of oblivion had been her goal and Jude had gladly obliged. This food-fest sexy time hadn't sprung from an emotional situation. It wasn't about her needing comfort and him wanting to provide it. They'd gone into this with no agenda and their eyes wide open.

And Clem didn't know what that meant.

Except this suddenly didn't feel black and white. It felt… blurry. Like maybe the situation had moved into a gray area where all kinds of possibilities lurked.

One thing was for sure, right here, right now wasn't the place for *that* discussion. With him still hard inside her and the sweet sticky residue of mousse still clinging to her skin.

"Or maybe we could... do that tomorrow?"

He grinned an utterly wolfish grin. "I like the way you think." He dropped his head and kissed her neck and the ridge of her collarbone and the hollow at the base of her throat. "Wrap your legs around me and hold on tight," he muttered, his warm breath creating delicious havoc.

Clem did as he asked, yelping a little as he scooped her off the counter then laughing against his mouth as he walked her to her bedroom. When they got to their destination, he eased her down onto the mattress withdrawing from her body at the last moment, an action that caused both to shudder.

"I'm going to turn the oven off," he said, his eyes raking over her body one last time as he backed out of the room. "Get naked."

He turned and was gone and Clem smiled as she stripped off her clothes, refusing to think beyond tonight to tomorrow, to their conversation and the possibilities that might be there if she opened herself up to the gray. Rhonda's voice whispered, *what if it didn't have to end?* and for the first time she asked herself the same question.

JUDE WAS ALSO trying not to think about tomorrow as he raced to his bedroom, dealt with the condom and shucked off his clothes. He had two weeks before he moved into his new rental and he didn't know what was going to happen next with him and Clementine. Did she want to move into a friend's-with-benefits setup for the remainder of his time here?

Did he?

Thinking about it rationally, if she'd been any other woman after something casual, Jude wouldn't have hesitated. But Clementine was the opposite of causal. More than that, they'd reconnected when they were both at a crossroads in their life. Not the best time to start something when they were heading in different directions.

If she wanted to boink like bunnies, Jude doubted he could say no because they were *good* together. And he hadn't been able to stop thinking about being with her again since that first time. But he'd be foolish to pretend their relationship hadn't moved beyond friends to some kind of *otherness*. Foolish to ignore the implications of pursing that too—both good and bad.

Because when he boiled it down, he knew he wanted Clementine in his life. They could be friends. They could be lovers. But could they be ex-lovers *and* friends?

That was the question.

Impatient with his thoughts, Jude pushed it all aside as he made a quick visit to the kitchen, switching the oven off and leaving the door slightly ajar for the pies to cool. As he turned, his gaze snagged on the piping bags loaded with chocolate mousse and he grinned.

Grabbing the fullest one, he departed with a spring in his step.

When he got to her bedroom she was lying naked in the center of the bed, and a sudden overwhelming feeling that she was *his* that she belonged to *him* sucker-punched him square in the gut. It was ridiculous—no one person *belonged* to another person—but *fuck*. The sudden riot of emotions clogging up his chest and lodging in his throat were utterly primal, catching him off guard with their intensity.

So much for thinking rationally.

"I see you are as instructed," he said, deliberately leering to cover his inner turmoil as he lingered in the doorway, the piping bag full of mousse behind his back.

"Well." She leered right back and Jude's dick responded predictably. "You'd ruined my sweater and undone my bra so the job was already half done."

"You're welcome."

She grinned. "Why are you standing all the way over there when its clear parts of your anatomy"—her gaze dropped to his excitable dick—"want you to be over here?"

"I was admiring the view."

"So am I. But it would be nice to admire it from a little closer, don't you think?"

Holy fuck yeah.

Jude entered the room, the hand with the piping bag casually situated behind his back. She sat, watching his progress, her breasts swinging enticingly as she wriggled to the edge of the mattress, her feet landing flat on the floor as he drew level. It was impossible *not* to notice that her mouth and his dick—which had clearly recovered very well from their countertop shenanigans—were temptingly close.

"Mmm," she said, her gaze taking its time to travel all

the way up his body before drifting back down again, stopping when it got to his erection.

Jude's balls tightened at the blatant hunger that dilated her pupils and flared her nostrils. A pulse thudded thick and slow at his groin. He swallowed. "Like what you see?"

"Oh yes."

Jude watched, his heart thumping like a gong, as her hand lifted and her fingertips tentatively touched down on the taut, aching flesh of his shaft. He sucked in a breath, his body swaying, his eyes shutting involuntarily for a moment at the exquisite torture of the barely there touch.

But he forced them open because he didn't want to miss a thing.

He wanted to watch her touch him. Watch as her hand wrapped around him, as her mouth explored him, as her lips stretched to accommodate him.

"Mmm," she said, her eyes lifting to him. "Is that what I think it is?"

It took Jude a beat or two to compute what she meant as her fingers lightly stroked up and down the length of his shaft. His hand had fallen to his side when his eyes had been shut and the piping bag was on full display.

"Yep."

"Oh, goody." She waggled her eyebrows at him, her hand sliding from his dick to claim the bag. "Or should I say—" She poised the nozzle above the hard jut of him. "Yummy?"

The muscles in his ass tightened as that nozzle hovered close. "I thought you weren't interested in piping?"

"It seems I just needed…" Her eyes zeroed in on the subject. "The right motivation."

Jude swallowed. He hadn't brought the bag from the kitchen for her use—he'd planned to demonstrate his artistic skills by making her into a piece of edible art—but Clementine was looking at his cock with serious purpose and he knew better than to stand in her way when she had that determined glean in her eyes.

"Well," he murmured, his voice husky. "In that case."

No sooner had the words left his mouth than a line of mousse was being piped from the center of his dick to the point where shaft met head and Jude's pulse skipped. But, when she put the bag down on the mattress, wrapped her hand around his lower half not covered in mousse and leaned in, it went haywire. Every muscle from his belly button to his thighs clenched tight in anticipation.

"*Mmm...* mint," she whispered as she kissed the tip, her tongue circling the slit. "You smell good."

Then her lips parted and her tongue circled lower, flicking the very edge of the mousse, and Jude watched as it retreated into her mouth, as her cheeks hollowed and she hummed her approval.

A noise that traveled like a thunderbolt down his shaft earthing in his balls.

She pulled back with a smile, her lips wet as they hovered a hair's breadth from the tip again. "You taste even better."

Then she opened her mouth and slowly and surely sucked him in. Jude groaned as the heat and the wet of her mouth surrounded him, the swirl of her tongue devouring the mousse and shredding any composure he'd been trying to maintain. Any pretence that he was in control flew out the window.

She might be in the position of supplicant but there was no doubt in his mind who held all the power. And this feeling he had for her, this... *need*... got stronger.

"Clementine," he muttered, shoving his hand into her hair, cradling her face, feeling her jaw working as his gut looped itself in knots.

She pulled away, the crown of his dick glistening as it *throbbed*, just in front of her lips, aching to be pleasured. "If you're still capable of talking," she said with a smile. "I must be doing this wrong."

Jude's thumb stroked along her cheekbone. "You're *not* doing it wrong."

"Then hush up and let me do my thing."

She grabbed the bag again and Jude chuckled and said, "Yes, chef," as more mousse was added and her tongue descended and he was lost.

AN HOUR LATER, after some very enthusiastic, very sticky sexual shenanigans, Jude was lying next to Clementine in the dark. She'd rolled onto her side and snuggled into his body, her head on his shoulder, her curls tickling his nose. Her top leg was draped over his thighs and Jude's hand held it there, spanning the spot just above her knee.

The aroma of pumpkin pies drifted into them as they chatted about Thanksgiving tomorrow, her fingers absently stroking the firm pads of his pecs.

It was... nice. And Jude didn't want it to end.

Cuddle time with women after sex had always felt performative to him because he'd never known any of them long enough or deep enough to take off his mask. The sex had been performative too because if they talked to the tabloids—and some of them had—then he didn't want a rep as a bad or inconsiderate lover. In bed with other women, he'd always been Jude Barlow celebrity chef and he'd felt the pressure to always be *on*.

He hadn't realized how much of a toll that had taken until spending these last couple of months with Clementine. With her, he was just *Jude*. He was the boy she met when she'd been eight. And she was the girl. She knew him down to his bones—he didn't need to pretend to be something else.

And it was fucking liberating!

He'd started that journey in Africa but Clementine had brought him all the way back to himself. She'd reintroduced him to the Jude he used to be—before the seduction of having his name in lights. She'd believed in his scattered, jet-lagged, half-assed plans because she'd listened to him prattle on about them for years back when he'd been a skinny kid with big ears and parents who fought all the time. And then she'd thrown down the gauntlet, challenging him to finally see them come to fruition, lecturing him on personal accomplishment.

Deep down, he must have suspected that she would and that was the true reason he'd sought her out in Marietta.

Whatever it was, Jude had a lot to thank Clementine for and perhaps that was what these deepening feelings were all about? Sure, there was that startling sexual connection that had whammied him in the gut earlier—but that was just physical.

There was *deeper* stuff, too. Like… thankfulness and appreciation. And *gratitude*.

He *owed* her for helping him make sense of his life and maybe these feelings were merely a reflection of that? She didn't *belong* to him in a *me Tarzan, you Jane* kind of way, more like she belonged to him in a way that had transcended friendship.

They belonged to each other.

"Mom's super excited for the stroll," Clementine said as Jude tuned back in to her lazy chatter. "It's still a couple of weeks away but if she isn't home by then we should be able to get her another day pass and a wheelchair. I think she quite relishes the idea of Dad pushing her down Main Street."

Her short sharp laugh puffed warm air near his nipple and shook through her whole body causing a delicious kind of friction between every part of her that was smooshed up against every part of him.

"I am too." He pulled lightly on one of her many springy curls, stretching it out before letting it go. "Everywhere I go people are talking about it."

"*I'm* excited for your first stroll." She shifted, propped herself up on her elbow and looked down at him. "The whole town comes alive and people come from all the surrounding areas to visit the stalls and see Santa and go on the hayrides. When I look back on my childhood, the strolls are some of my happiest memories."

Her eyes practically glowed and his breath hitched. She

was utterly incandescent.

Suddenly a burst of Beyoncé broke the air. "Oops, sorry. That's Merridy's ringtone. She's one of my Contiki friends. They all got back yesterday. Do you mind if I take it?"

"Of course not."

Rolling away from him, she groped in her bag on the bedside table then flopped onto her back as she answered. Jude bent his arm and shoved it under his head as he listened in the dark to her chat with her friend about her mom then quizzed her about the trip without so much as a trace of envy. Considering she'd missed out on an eight-week dream vacation to the Mediterranean, she'd be entitled to feel that way a little.

"Japan? When? How long?" Jude's stomach tightened at the breathy little hitch to her voice. "Three weeks. In April? Um… yeah… I'd love to but I'm just not sure… Everything should be okay with Mom by then, fingers crossed, but my friend Sondra has some more feelers out for me in New York so I might actually be employed then. When would you need to know by?"

And that was the moment. Lying here, listening to her make plans that *did not include him*—when they'd spent the last two months practically in each other's pockets—that was the moment he realized those feelings he'd analyzed a few minutes ago.

That was utter bullshit. What he'd been feeling wasn't fucking *gratitude*. It was *love*. Jude's heart almost punched through his ribs it was banging so damn hard at the revelation. *Transcended friendship?* Oh, Jesus… what an idiot.

He'd fallen in *love* with her.

This thing he was feeling, as he listened to her causally talk about leaving to go to New York and on vacation to Japan, was like an axe to his fucking heart. Like he was being peeled open. He was overwhelmed with how much he wanted to hold her, wrap her up, and never ever let her go. It boiled like a fever in his blood.

Yeah... not gratitude. Definitely not *friendship*, either. He loved her.

It rose up like a tide now, filling every nook and cranny in his body from his toes to the tips of his hair. Every cell, every vein, every single cavity. And all the empty spaces that had formed over the years that he'd filled with *stuff* hoping it would be enough.

Love coursed like a river—true and deep and sure.

And she was planning her life without him. Of course she was. And, with a hot, sinking feeling in his gut he knew he *wasn't* going to wrap her up, he was going to have to sit back and wait and hope and be her goddamn *friend*, existing in that space, because she'd been on the cusp of all this when they'd reconnected and she *deserved* to have it all. He was finally living his dreams—what kind of an asshole would he be to begrudge her, hers?

If you loved something you set it free, right? Even if it killed him in the process.

And in the meantime he'd follow his path. Establish the inn. Work on *him*. Follow his dream and make it happen as she had urged him the fateful night of her birthday party. And maybe, one day, if he was lucky, she might come back to him.

"Sorry about that."

Clementine rolled away, placing her phone on the bedside table and Jude stared at the the length of her spine and the curve of an ass cheek as the sheet slipped.

"Japan, huh?" He kept his voice even as she joined him, snuggling into his side.

Jude shut his eyes and reveled in the heat and press of her as his arm curled around her shoulder and a sense of rightness pervaded every inch of his body.

Christ, how had he been so blind?

"I don't know... maybe, if it works out. There's too many variables at the moment. Mom and New York. Sondra called a few days ago about the possibility of short-term contract work at the Met so I guess it could all come together?" She shook her head and her curls tickled his nose. "It would be awesome if it did. I've always wanted to go to Japan."

"It's an amazing place. And April is cherry blossom season, which is breathtaking."

She levered herself up on her elbow again, her hair falling forward in a springy mass as she looked down at him. "You've been?"

Jude pushed back the curls. She looked so earnest and eager and his heart squeezed. "Yeah, I've done some celebrity chef stuff there over the years."

She sighed. "You're so lucky."

He had been lucky. He'd been blessed. Sure, he'd gotten burned out and lost sight of what was important, but there'd been so much good stuff, too. But that wasn't for now. Right now, he was in bed with the woman he loved and while he might not be able to tell her that, he sure as *fuck* could show her.

In the morning, they'd have that talk and he'd distance himself with some bullshit about the importance of their friendship but they still had tonight.

"You have no idea," he said, his fingers trailing down her cheek, over her lips to her jaw. Then, lunging, he flipped her, Clementine laughing as she landed on her back.

"That's a slick move," she murmured as he settled between her thighs.

Jude nuzzled her ear. "Plenty more where that came from."

And he proceeded to show her.

Chapter Ten

THE AROMA OF roasting chestnuts and hot dogs spiced the air as Jude stood on the steps of the courthouse along with his fellow finalists. Behind them in the distance, the looming shape of Copper Mountain stood sentinel over Marietta and all the stroll festivities currently underway. On this cold, crisp, Saturday evening, the snowy peak stood out, ghostlike before it ceded farther downhill to the dark shapes of evergreen conifers, starkly outlined by the three-quarter moon.

Laid out in front of him, the historic hub of downtown Marietta had been transformed into a magical Christmas fair with street vendors selling their wares from hot chocolate and mulled wine to arts and crafts. There were family groups everywhere and the murmur of conversation and laughter mixed with the jingle of sleigh bells and the clopping of horse's hooves as the hayride picked up more customers. Little pink-cheeked children ate cotton candy with one hand and clutched their precious free photo with Santa they'd had taken in the foyer of the Graff in the other.

Main Street, which was perennially picture-postcard pretty had taken on an extra festive glow. Santa had not long ago led the lighting ceremony and the Christmas lights that had been installed over the past few days had taken everything from merry to radiant with the flick of the ceremonial switch. Even the courthouse façade behind him twinkled gaily.

"And the winner is..."

The food critic judge from Helena—a man called Charles—addressed the crowd at the foot of the courthouse steps. The towns' category had already been announced and Marietta's mayor had accepted the plaque in front of the cheering crowd of mostly Marietta locals. Now it was the individual category and Jude stood beside a woman who owned a bakery in Livingstone and a restaurateur from Bozeman.

"Go, Jude," Vivian called, which was followed quickly by shouts of support from all around.

Sage, who was standing right beside Vivian, threw in her two cents. "You've got this in the bag, Jude!"

He grinned at them. Their amazing displays had played no small part in Marietta taking out the towns' category. Viv had arranged hundreds of *Delish's* signature golden wrapped chocolate bars into a magnificent Christmas tree and lit it up with what seemed like a thousand lights. And Sage had used Lego people and her fantastic specialized chocolates to create a replica Santa's workshop.

But the well wishes were not all for him. There were also people from Livingstone and Bozeman and the other surrounding towns in the audience who were equally boisterous with their support.

Clementine was standing next to Edwin and, as his gaze met hers, she shot him the thumbs-up. She looked so damn cute, her hands clasped around a take-out cup of *Delish* hot chocolate, her chipmunk cheeks all rosy and that silly knit cap with the kitten ears pulled down low on her forehead containing all the springy wildness beneath.

He wanted to laugh out loud but hell if he didn't also want to throw himself down on his knees in front of her and declare how much he loved her in front of the whole damn town. Given the very public rebuff he'd had last time he'd attempted something similar, Jude suppressed the urge.

Thankfully, after their night together, she'd accepted his suggestion they stick with being friends and they'd moved quickly past the next day awkwardness. It helped, he supposed that it hadn't been their first rodeo but still, these past couple of weeks hadn't been easy. Being so close, sharing so much with her in their cozy domestic setting—eating, chatting, watching the TV, sharing the minutiae of their day as snow fell outside and they folded those goddamn paper cranes—and not being free to touch and to hold and to kiss and to tell her how he felt?

That had been *hard*.

So many times, they'd been laughing over something and it had been on the tip of his tongue to tell her—to tell all. But the words had seized in his throat because as tortuous as it was to love her and keep it a secret, confession wasn't in the cards.

He didn't want to be *that* guy. The one that put himself and his needs and wants first. Especially when he knew Clementine had bigger dreams than Marietta.

"For their magnificent chocolate gingerbread village, it's the Graff Hotel."

The crowd went wild, all leaping up and down and hugging each other and Jude grinned as he accepted the congratulations of his fellow competitors and Charles who handed a large cup made from chocolate and wrapped in golden foil. He held it above his head good-naturedly much to the delight of the assembled, and then he and his fellow finalists, and Edwin and Charles, all posed for a picture snapped by a photographer from the local paper.

But throughout it all, he was really only conscious of one person—Clementine—beaming up at him, waiting patiently among the crowd at the bottom of the steps as they all surged forward to congratulate him. It took him almost ten minutes—*ten* long minutes—before he got to her and she didn't disappoint, throwing herself at him enthusiastically.

"You did it, Jude," she said, her voice muffled in his neck.

She pulled away and kissed him just as enthusiastically. Just a peck. A quick congratulatory press of her lips—that was all. But it spoke of a deeper level of intimacy between them. It was the kind of kiss lovers gave to one another in greeting. And it simultaneously clutched at his groin and squeezed warm fingers around his heart.

It was moments like this he actually looked forward to moving out on Monday, knowing he wouldn't have to constantly battle these feelings.

There was a split second of awkwardness as she clearly realized what she'd done—kissed him on the mouth in front of everyone—their gazes not quite meeting, but then Edwin joined them for another round of congratulations and the moment passed.

"Thanks," Jude said as Edwin shook his hand again. "I think I did Marietta proud."

"Are you kidding?" Clementine grinned and it practically stole his breath. "Marietta's going to *adopt* you."

"If they don't," Edwin said, clapping him on the back, "I will."

They spoke briefly about work in the morning before Edwin moved away and Jude turned his attention to Clementine who was smiling at him, the epitome of smugness. "I told you you'd win."

The utter faith blazing from her amber eyes set the emotions in his chest ajumble and he pushed them determinedly aside. "You haven't even seen it yet." He'd completed the chocolate gingerbread village five days ago but Clementine had been holding out for the stroll to see it.

"I was waiting until it was award-winning."

"Well—" He handed her the cup. "You were right."

"I never doubted it." She admired the gaudy trophy. "Okay, let's go." She handed him back the cup. "Take me to your village."

"Yes ma'am."

CLEM SMILED AT the carolers serenading passersby just outside the grand entrance of the Graff. "Oh, Come All Ye Faithful" accompanied her and Jude into the foyer and a surge of town pride and Christmas joy mixed in Clem's chest to put her in an oddly nostalgic mood.

So much so that she almost burst into tears when she saw

Jude's chocolate gingerbread village given pride of place in the middle of the gift shop. The Graff hosted a gingerbread competition every year, which were currently displayed in many of the shop windows around Marietta. A chocolate twist on that had been utterly inspired.

"Oh, Jude." She clutched her chest as she gazed upon his masterpiece. "It's…" She glanced at him, shaking her head, and he was looking at her with such *intensity*, she couldn't look away.

But she had to, because her eyes were stinging from the effort of suppressing the threatening tears. Blinking them away, she turned her attention to the village again not that she took much in as her brain tried to figure out what the hell was wrong with her. She'd been feeling weird since she accidentally kissed him on the mouth earlier—sure, it had only been a peck, but it hadn't been her intention. She'd been going for his cheek. A congratulatory kiss between friends but the brief press of their lips had felt way more… intimate somehow.

She felt like they'd gotten past any morning-after weirdness from their chocolate mousse-inspired sex marathon the night before Thanksgiving but now it was like she was right back there again. Awkward over a kiss. And crying. Over a chocolate gingerbread village?

What in hell was the matter with her?

Sure, it was beautiful, with the intricate white frosting giving each house a regal kind of elegance. The color and gaudiness of the commercially bought candy embellishments were a stark contrast but even they were precisely cut and perfectly placed. Nothing ramshackle or haphazard—

everything was neat and regimented. The tidiest of tidy chocolate gingerbread towns complete with chocolate houses, chocolate trees, chocolate roads, chocolate hedges and chocolate lightposts.

It had taken him many man hours to construct and Clem could see why. She could also see why he'd taken the grand prize. But, it wasn't worth crying over, surely?

Although works of art did inspire high emotion, right? She remembered staring up at the ceiling of the Sistine Chapel, marvelling at its magnificence with tears falling down her cheeks. If she added in the nostalgia of the stroll, nearly losing her mom not long ago, and the occasional drift of traditional Christmas carols from outside, it was a *lot*.

No wonder she was a little emotional.

"It's?" he prompted, coming to stand near her elbow.

Clem cleared her throat of the lump pressing on her vocal chords. "Amazing," she said then forced herself to look at him and smile normally and stop being such a freaking *dork*. "Of course, you won the competition, it's absolutely exquisite."

Pricking at the backs of her eyes warned of another stealth attack by her tear ducts and Clem quickly returned her gaze to the village.

"Yeah, gotta admit, I impressed even myself."

"Well, that is high praise," Clem said, forcing a light teasing note into her voice.

He laughed. "I am my own harshest critic…"

"Aren't we all?" she murmured, risking a glance at him.

He looked at her at the same time and smiled and she smiled back and the strange vibe evaporated and they were just two friends again sharing their evening together.

"Oh wow, Mommy!" A little girl pulled up beside them looking a little like the Michelin Man in her puffy jumpsuit, a knit hat with a pom-pom on top pulled down over her ears. She looked about five or six and stared at the chocolate village before her with awe and wonder. "Is it *all* made of chocolate?"

Clem didn't recognize the mother who smiled at them politely before answering her daughter. "Yep, all of it."

"Are we allowed to eat it?"

"Definitely not."

Undeterred the little girl shifted tack. "Can we jump in? Like Mary Poppins did with Bert and live in there forever?"

The mom laughed and Clem bit the inside of her cheek to prevent herself from following suit. Jude grinned from ear to ear as she said, "No, darling, we can't."

"Can we make one at home?"

"Umm." The woman looked it over clearly intimidated. "Sure. Something like it anyway." She held out her hand. "C'mon, let's go. We gotta meet up with your cousin for the hayride."

They departed then and Clem turned to him. "*Are* we allowed to eat it?" she asked, a smile on her mouth.

Jude laughed. "Definitely not."

Clem sighed. "Spoilsport."

But he just grinned and said, "Fancy a hayride?"

"Well, it's not eating an entire chocolate village, but it'll do." Any distraction from this damn mood bringing her down tonight would do.

They exited the Graff and headed for the courthouse

again. Clem was very aware of Jude beside her, their arms occasionally brushing as they walked. "I'm going to see another property that's just come on the market tomorrow. You want to come?"

"Sure," she said, absently.

"If you don't want to, it's okay."

She crinkled her brow at him. "I want to." Clem enjoyed accompanying Jude on his property viewings, she was just feeling kinda weird right now. "I'll miss doing it when you move out."

Aaand there went her mood again—nose-diving off a cliff. She'd buried herself in Jude's research and meetings with the occupational therapist regarding the modifications to her mom and dad's house that were required for Trina's eventual return, all of which had allowed Clem to push Jude's impending departure to the back of her mind.

But he was moving into his rental on *Monday*.

Clem loved living by herself—she loved the freedom to be herself, she loved having a place to call her own. But, having Jude around these past couple of months had been... well, she didn't want to analyze it too hard but it had been unexpectedly easy.

Jude had *fit*. And she didn't want to analyze *that* either.

"You can still come with me," he said. "Whenever you're free."

Clem blinked. Maybe it was the cold air but he sounded kind of gruff all of a sudden. "I'd like that." She nodded. "Thanks."

"Of course," he dismissed and it definitely sounded gruff this time.

Freaking hell—they were a fine pair tonight. Trying to shake the mood off once again, she elbowed him. "I'll also miss your cooking."

For some reason, Clem's brain didn't go to the dozens and dozens of scrumptious meals he had made for her—and her father—these past two months. It went straight to chocolate mousse. To eating chocolate mousse of him.

To *him* eating it off *her*.

Ugh... do not think about that night right now. She could think about it tonight all alone in bed and god knew how many other nights in the future but not when they were walking side by side down Main Street, Marietta, where half the people who had known her since she was a baby were out and about and probably reading her freaking mind.

Thankfully *he* didn't go there, although his voice did sound husky as he said, "I'm sure you'll survive, Clementine Jones."

Nearby sleigh bells drifted to them and Clem leapt at their intrusion. "Quick," she said, picking up the pace, "we don't want to miss the next ride."

Because right now an itchy, boisterous ride with a bunch of raucous families was far preferable to thinking about Monday.

CLEM FOLDED THE one thousandth paper crane in the car the next day on the way to see the latest property Jude was inspecting. She'd done a count when she'd gone to bed last night because she knew they must be close. Turned out, they'd been at nine hundred and eighty-one and she'd folded eighteen more this morning in between printing and filing about two dozen recipes she'd just stumbled upon on an obscure website to do with wagon wheels.

Jude had spent his usual few hours at the Graff and picked her up at eleven as she was about to start the final one and there was no way she was leaving it, so she'd brought it with her. Jude had laughed and accused her of being obsessed, which was fairly accurate but, she'd realized it was the perfect leaving gift for him.

Given how many hours they'd worked on the project together it was fitting. More than that, it was symbolic of *them*. The them they'd been all those years ago and the them they were now.

Paper cranes, it seemed, had always connected them.

It took her longer than it normally did to fold one because he was telling her all about the dozens of congratulatory phone calls Edwin had taken since last night and then he asked her what she thought about him doing a cookbook, a chocolate based one, and her fingers stopped folding altogether.

"Seriously?" she asked.

"Yeah." He nodded. "Edwin suggested it and I don't know… it's growing on me."

"It must have been suggested to you before?" It seemed like every celebrity chef these days put out a cookbook.

"I have been approached in the past, yes. I was just busy… there didn't seem time to do something like that."

"Well, there you go then. You have plenty time now, right? I think it's a *brilliant* idea."

"You do?"

He grinned and it just about stopped the breath in Clem's lungs, which caused a cramp in her chest. *Damn it.* She'd woken this morning after a solid eight hours sleep with her weird mood from last night lifted and she'd felt *good* about the future. Positive. About the strength of their friendship and how much they both had to look forward to in their lives going forward.

But now, in the confines of the car, her chest felt tight and the air was suddenly stuffy.

"Yes." She nodded enthusiastically ignoring her body which was being utterly ridiculous. "I'd buy it in a heartbeat."

He chuckled. "You would, huh?"

"Yep."

"And then make me cook something out of it for you?"

"Of course. What's the point in having one of the country's most well-known chefs as a friend if I can't use it to my advantage?" she teased, lightly. But it cost her. Pricks of pain stabbed her at her chest, like pins being driven into her heart.

"It'd be a great project to work on while I'm getting the inn established."

"It'd be perfect," Clem agreed.

They chatted a bit more about that while Clem finished her crane. When it was done she popped it in the pocket of her hoodie for safekeeping. He was going straight from the Graff to the rental tomorrow so she'd give it to him in the morning before she left for work.

Which she was *not* going to think about now.

They'd been traveling for almost half an hour when Jude

saw the sign indicating the next small town was five miles away. "Not far now. It's just a mile or so outside of Emigrant."

"Do you know which side of the road?"

"No."

Up ahead, through a small thicket of trees on the right-hand side of the road, Clem glimpsed two red gables. She pointed. "That must be it there."

Jude slowed and crossed to the other side, coasting to a halt in front of the prominent FOR SALE sign. Goose bumps broke out along Clem's scalp as he switched off the engine and they both just sat and stared.

It was nothing big or spectacular or grand and it clearly needed some TLC but there were snow-covered mountains behind in the distance and it was surrounded by trees—bare for now, but they'd be back come spring. Garden beds lined the neat front path. They needed some loving also as did the wraparound porch and the roof and the blue front door could do with a lick of paint. Hell, it all could.

But everything about the building *beckoned*. Clem felt its welcome right down to her bones. "Oh, Jude," she murmured.

He nodded and turned his head to face her. "*That's* what I'm talking about."

Then he opened his door and disembarked, not even grabbing his jacket from the back seat. Clem picked it up as she retrieved hers—it was freezing outside today. Catching him in the middle of the path, she handed it over to him. He didn't say anything as they shrugged into their jackets, just stood and stared with a faraway look in his eyes.

She had the feeling he was in Texas somewhere, caught in a memory and even though her heart throbbed in her chest and she wanted to slip her hand into his and be in it with him, she also didn't want to disturb.

Zipping his jacket, he finally moved on, up the path then up the front porch steps, stopping to look around, putting his hands on the railing and surveying the large front area as if he was already making plans for it. Then he moved to the door, fishing in the front pocket of his jeans for the key then sliding it in.

The door opened easily and the tears came again as Clem stepped into the large open room, wide oak floorboards beneath her feet, decorative ceilings soaring overhead and light flooding in from the line of French doors opposite.

This was it, she realized. She was standing in it—right in the middle of Jude's dream. And the truly wrenching part of it was that she wanted to be in it *with him* so bad she could barely breath.

Oh, dear god… what was happening to her? This wasn't her dream. It was Jude's. She *did not* want to live in a freaking inn in the middle of nowhere. New York beckoned. Japan beckoned. The *world* beckoned.

So why did it feel like her heart was trying to thump its way out of her chest?

Luckily, Jude was oblivious to her inner turmoil as he trailed from room to room trancelike, his hand absently running over surfaces, his eyes darting over windows and ceilings and floors as if he was already mentally furnishing the empty spaces. Everything was old and a little neglected but that feeling he'd talked about—it was in every inch of this place.

Clem knew it and she knew he knew it, too.

When he was done inside and, still without a word passing between them, he headed for the French doors, unlocking the catch on the middle set and pushing them open. Clem followed him as he stepped out onto the back porch and repeated what he'd done on the front porch, placed his hands on the railing and inspected the land.

There was a large area of what would just be lawn when the weather grew warmer before several boxed garden beds, which were currently fallow. Beyond that was some more lawn, a greenhouse that needed work and then about a dozen trees, probably only as tall as Jude and mostly bare of leaves. They looked old though—the branches all gnarled and intertwined.

"Oh, my god," Jude said, pushing away from the railing and hurrying to the porch steps.

Clem watched as his long-legged stride took him across the yard, passed the boxed beds and the greenhouse and straight to a tree toward the back that she couldn't see well from her vantage point. He plucked something off a branch before heading back again, his warmth breath misting into the cold air as he grinned at her.

She couldn't help but grin back. Jude was good-looking at the best of times but with that big ol' smile, he was *sexy*. Taking the four porch steps two at a time, he brandished his treasure.

"Is that an apple?" she asked as he approached.

"Yes, ma'am, it is." He came to a stop in front of her. "Hold out your hand."

Clem rolled her eyes but she held it out and he placed his find in the center. It was cold in her palm and small, also quite shriveled. But it was most definitely an apple.

"It's an orchard," he said unnecessarily, his face practically aglow with the discovery. "It'll need a bit of tending to but…" He grinned. "I have an apple orchard."

Clem's heart just about burst with the pride and possession in his voice, as if he'd given *birth* to the damn thing. "*You* have an orchard, huh?" she teased because if she didn't the sudden tightness in her throat might take over.

He nodded. "I do now."

Clem looked down at the apple in her palm. It didn't look remotely inviting and she sure as shit wasn't going to take a bite of it but a *surge* of tears welled then and it didn't matter how much she swallowed and blinked to halt their progress, they were unstoppable.

This was Jude's apple. And she wanted it to be hers, too. Because, goddamn it, she loved this man. She was *in love* with Jude Barlow—childhood friend, celebrity chef, roomie.

The feelings from last night, the ones that had been growing and growing and she'd been ignoring—they weren't nostalgia or a result of him being here for her when she needed him or all the stress she'd been under.

This was *love*.

From the moment he'd arrived presenting her with an engagement ring to this moment presenting her with an *apple*, he had become such an integral part of her life. She couldn't even pinpoint a moment when she'd fallen for him, it just glowed in her chest with sudden clarity and certainty.

Big and inescapable and so freaking inconvenient.

She'd always assumed love, when it happened, would come in like wrecking ball. *Thank you, Miley Cyrus.* She hadn't realized it could launch a stealth attack. That it would tiptoe into her life and her heart and take over slowly and gently and surely until it built to the point of undeniable.

Unable to stem the tears any longer, one escaped, plopping down onto the ruched red skin. It was useless to hope he hadn't seen it considering he was looking at the damn apple like he was about to write it into his will.

"Clementine?" His voice was low and urgent as he plucked it out of her hand. "What's wrong?"

She shook her head, turning away from him, placing her hands on the cold railing again. "Nothing."

But he followed, standing beside her, his body turned into her, his belly pressing into her elbow. "Why are you crying?"

"I'm fine." She shook her head as she cleared her throat. "It's just beautiful is all."

"The apple?"

If Clem hadn't been so close to losing it, she'd have laughed at the incredulous streak in his voice. "Yes."

He snorted. "This is my apple and I love it but it is the sorriest, most butt-ugly looking apple I've ever seen, Clementine, so cut the bullshit. What's wrong?"

She turned away as two more tears fell. "It's freezing out here," she said, heading for the relative warmth and distance of inside, dashing at the tears as she went.

"Clementine," he called after her but she wasn't stopping, striding across the room that would be so beautiful once Jude had done it up and not stopping.

He was hot on her heels though, catching her up near the door which she got open about an inch before he put his hand up high on the wood, shutting it again. "I'm fine, Jude," she said, choking on a sob, pressing her forehead to the back of the door, aware, as his warmth surrounded her, of how close he was behind.

God she was dissolving at a rate of knots now, her heart beating frantically. It seemed the more she tried to pull herself together, the more she fell apart.

"You're not," he growled, his breath ruffling her hair. "Please." The hand he had up high slid down the door to her shoulder. "Turn around. Please talk to me."

Clementine swallowed the urge to stay where she was and just sob but it was bad enough she was crying, he didn't need the whole snot crying mess. She scrubbed at her tears and turned, prepared to fob him off with anything but the truth. Anything to put him off so she could get out and away and regroup.

Think about this for a moment devoid from the rawness of her discovery.

She must have looked a right mess though, Jude's entire face creasing in concern. "Oh god, Clementine." He leaned in and kissed her forehead, his body brushing lightly against her which only made her want to cry further. "What's wrong?" He cupped her face. "Why are you crying?"

Her throat itched and her nose was already runny and she sniffled. She opened her mouth to tell him she was worried about her mom or how her funds were starting to run low and she might have to go back to the library in the new year but that wasn't what she said.

"Because I don't want you to move out."

Which was utterly preposterous—it would take her less than five minutes to drive to his place. Ten if she walked. But the thought that she'd come home and he wouldn't be there waiting for her like the last two months was almost unbearable. Another hot tear spilled from the corner of her eye and slid down the side of his face before his thumb wiped it away.

"Okay. Why don't you want me to move out?"

"Because I—" Clem stalled as her brain worked through several possibilities—all of them unsubstantial. She shook her head. "I... can't." She dropped her gaze to his throat. "I can't tell you."

"Hey," he whispered, his finger sliding under her chin and raising it until she was looking at him through her wet spiky eyelashes. He smiled gently. "I love you. You can tell me anything."

Clementine blinked. Slowly at first then more rapidly as she tried to compute what he'd just said. He loved her? "Wh...what?"

"I said"—he leaned in close, his lips grazing close to her ear—"I'm in love with you."

"But..."

He drew back, his mouth curving into a slow smile. "No buts."

Her pulse fluttered madly at all her pulse points. "You... do?"

"I do."

"Since when?"

"Well... I think being honest, it was probably eighteen

years ago but I finally realized a couple of weeks ago after we… made love." He said the words slowly as if trying it on for size and liking it very much if his smile was anything to go by. "And you were on the phone to Merridy making plans for Japan. Without me even being a consideration and it just whammied me from out of the blue."

Oh god… she remembered that conversation, she hadn't thought about him at all. Just herself. "*Right*." Emotion overwhelmed her and her face crumpled again. "Exactly."

"Exactly?" He frowned. "Why don't you want me to move out, Clementine?"

"Because I love you, too, damnit," she said on a sob as she pushed against his body. When he stepped aside she paced to the middle of the room, tears streaming.

"That's making you miserable?" He laughed. "Isn't that a good thing?"

"No." She turned to face him not even caring what kind of hot mess she looked like now because he loved her and she loved him and *still* they couldn't be.

"Why?"

"Because we're at different stages of our life, Jude. You've had all your travel and adventures and now you want to settle somewhere and put down roots. I've done all the staid sensible career-orientated things and now I want to live a little. I want adventures."

He leaned casually against the door, a *V* between his brows. "You think I'm going to stop you doing that?"

"No. I'm worried about *me* stopping *me* from doing it because now I want this damn inn too and that"—she pointed at his hand—"damn apple and you in my damn bed in my damn house every night."

"Really?" His mouth curved into a smile.

Clem folded her arms. "I'm being serious, Jude Barlow."

He chuckled as he pushed off the door and walked slowly in her direction. "You used to say exactly that when we were kids. With your arms folded, too."

"We are not kids, anymore."

Eyes looked her slowly up and down as he approached and her jeans felt like they'd been set on fire. "Hallelujah," he murmured as he pulled up in front of her.

"*Jude.*"

Sighing, he tentatively slipped his hand onto her arm. "Clementine. I love you. You love me. I'm an ex-celebrity chef who is opening an inn in Montana and writing a cookbook. You're a small-town librarian with her eye on the Big Apple and a hankering to travel. Do those things have to be mutually exclusive?"

Even through the layers of her coat and her hoodie and the long-sleeved blouse she wore beneath it all, Clem swore she could feel the imprint of his hand and it made her *dizzy*. Too dizzy to think straight and she stepped back. "Yes?"

"Why can't you have both?"

Clem frowned. "What?"

"You want to go to New York and work? Go to New York and work—we'll commute."

She gaped at him. "Commute?"

"I'm rich." He shrugged. "We'll figure it out. And you know, we could travel together, if you wanted? There's places in this world I'd really like to show you."

Travel with Jude? Clem couldn't think of anything she

wanted more. *God*, the idea was so damn seductive. But she'd been around long enough to know how demanding a business could be especially when it was first being established.

"What about the inn?" she demanded. "You're not going to be able to drop that and just go galivanting off around the world."

"Spontaneous travel will be hard, sure, but we can open seasonally which would leave plenty of opportunity to travel. And I'll make sure to train a good manager from the get-go. Someone who can step in and take over when we're away. Yes, this is my dream, but I've already let one business rule my life, I'm not up for that again."

Clem thought he had a lot to learn about the employment landscape in rural Montana but his *when we're away* was super distracting. She shut her eyes for a second and let herself believe they could have that life. Opening them again, she found him studying her, his gorgeous whiskery face a picture of calm and patience. "I'm *not* going to marry you."

He laughed. "I don't recall asking but, okay."

She quirked an eyebrow. "Yeah, well, given your track record, I felt it was worth mentioning."

Pressing his lips together, he nodded. "Fair enough. Just… out of curiosity, why aren't you marrying me?"

"Babies."

"Okay…"

"All my friends get married and they say they're not having babies for five or ten years and guess what? Within a year, it's all they talk about." Not to mention how relentless her mom would be. "And within two, *pop*!"

Trying not to laugh, he pressed his lips together a little harder. "You do know you can get pregnant when you're not married, right?"

Yes, damn it, she knew that. But she already wanted this inn and that apple and him, so who knew how much ground she might give? "Not me."

"Okay." He nodded. "So, just to clarify, you *don't* want babies?"

"I…" She faltered. Damn it, she couldn't say categorically that she didn't want them *ever*. Just not now. "Maybe. I don't know. One day."

"Yeah…" He smiled gently. "I think that would be okay. One day."

"But *not* in the foreseeable future."

"Agreed."

"Promise me," she said, her gaze meeting with his and locking. "Promise me you *won't* ask me to marry you."

She was taking a leap of faith, grabbing hold of both things she wanted—adventure *and* Jude—and hoping it would be all right. She needed to know he was on the same page.

Reaching out, he took her cold hand with his big warm one and brought it to his chest. "I promise not to marry you, Clementine Jones. I promise not to *ask* you to marry me. I promise not to even *think* about asking you to marry me."

Another stupid lump rose in her throat. In this big empty shell of a building that still somehow hummed with warmth and life and would one day be the inn of Jude's dreams, she'd never heard anything so damn romantic. "Good."

"Now—" He grinned. "Can we skip ahead to the bit where we tell each other we love each other and we'll never let each other go then make out a little?"

Clem's heart bloomed like freaking *spring* in her chest as she stepped right into his arms and she was reminded of Tasmin and the way she'd looked at Gary on their wedding day. Like he was *the one* and nothing else mattered.

And that was how she felt about Jude. "I love you, Jude and I'm never letting you go."

He slid a hand either side of her face, looking at her like she was *the one* and nothing else mattered. Like she was all he'd ever need. "I love you, Clementine and I'm never letting you go."

Then he kissed her, deep and slow and if she hadn't understood the depth of his feelings already, she did now, his kiss a pledge, leaving no room for doubt. And she returned the favor, giving him her pledge in the most primal of ways. When they finally pulled apart, they were panting hard, their foreheads pressing together as they caught their breath.

"So," Clem said easing away from him when she was in control enough to speak and looking around. "This is it, huh? The one?"

"Yup. Can't you feel it too?"

She lifted her hand to the soft bristles covering his jaw. "I can." She glanced out the window at the orchard and saw all the cobbler Jude could make. "What are you going to call it?" she asked returning her attention to him.

"I've been thinking about stuff that has significance from my childhood, maybe to do with the inn we stayed at during my dad's bird-watching trips. Or from camp?"

A sudden thought pinged into Clem's mind. She unzipped her jacket and put her hand into her hoodie pocket and pulled out the origami she'd folded in the car and handed it over. "How about the Paper Crane?"

He took it from her fingers, turning it over and over, his smile growing bigger and bigger. "Yes." He glanced at her. "I *love* it. And I love you." He kissed her then stealing her breath. "It's perfect."

She smiled, the room spinning a little. "This is number one thousand," she said retrieving the crane to admire her handiwork. "You get to make a wish now and it'll come true."

Slowly, he shook his head. "I don't need it. I have everything I want right here."

And, as he kissed her again, dipping her in his arms, Clementine could not have agreed more.

Epilogue

Eighteen months later...

CLEM COULDN'T BELIEVE how fast the months had flown as she stood in the beautifully refurbished Paper Crane which had opened for business six months ago. Low murmurs from the gathered crowd rose up to the high ceiling and floated in from the overflow of people who had spilled out onto the back porch through the open French doors.

She stood side by side with Jude, his arm around her waist, in the central living room between two tables. One held an array of gourmet delights—including apple cobbler—all cooked by Jude and waiting to be consumed, the other boasted artfully arranged piles of his new cookbook—*You Had Me at Chocolate*.

Jude had accomplished a lot in such a short period of time and Clem was so proud. So, also had she, working in New York for nine months last year first for the Met on a short-term contract followed by six months with another art dealer friend of Eliza's on the provenance of some eighteenth-century paintings.

Then, as the inn renovation was in full swing and Jude had started work on the cookbook she had joined him as his principle researcher—paid by the publishing company. Clem had absolutely adored the experience and his publisher had been so impressed with her meticulous work that they'd offered her as much freelance work as she wanted on a variety of different projects.

Life was freaking *great*!

Gently, she tapped a knife against the side of her champagne glass, the *tinking* noise calling everyone to order. "Thank you all for coming here today," Clem said, addressing what felt like half of Marietta. "We'll be in New York tomorrow night celebrating the official launch of Jude's cookbook and then away on a two-month book tour through America, Europe, and Asia."

She was still pinching herself over that and so thankful that Jude had been true to his word about employing a manager. Julieann Lindsay had been an absolute godsend and she winked at Clem from the crowd.

"But," she continued, "both he and I wanted to celebrate here with all our friends from Marietta first."

The clapping and cheering became almost deafening then and she paused, grinning at the spectacle. Clem's proud parents beamed at her. Her mom was almost fully recovered from her stroke. There was some residual weakness in her left leg but it caused only minimal disruption to her mobility.

She only occasionally mentioned grandbabies.

Jude's parents were also here and just as obviously proud of their son's accomplishments. His father had been super thrilled over Jude's choice of name for the inn.

"I think it's fair to say that in the short eighteen months Jude has been a part of Marietta life, he has made quite a splash. From a rash public marriage proposal—" Laughter and some heckling followed and Clem grinned. "To a quickie wedding cake people are still talking about."

From somewhere outside Tamsin called, "Best damn cake ever," and there was more laughter.

"To wowing anyone who's ever eaten dessert at the Graff."

"Best damn restaurant ever," Edwin said, mimicking Tamsin to further hilarity.

"To the opening of this amazing inn and now this—" Clem reached over and plucked a book off the pile, holding it up.

"*You Had Me at Chocolate*," Clem continued, "is the most beautiful cookbook you will ever own."

"All thanks to Clementine," Jude interrupted, raising a glass in her direction.

The assembled crowd all clapped and Clem smiled at her gorgeous man and thanked god he'd stumbled into Marietta that night and proposed to her. "It is crammed with Jude's amazing chocolate recipes and the most gorgeous pictures. Trust me, you're going to want to lick the pages."

More laughter and applause followed and Jude leaned in and murmured, "Speaking of, there is some mousse left over in the fridge for later," against her temple.

Clem's belly clenched at the wicked suggestion as her brain calculated how long it would be before they could move this crowd on and be alone.

"So... grab your copy, the chef will even sign it if you want."

"I will," Jude confirmed.

"Then eat up and drink up and thank you all for coming."

The crowd surged forward and Clem moved out of the way as Jude was surrounded by people wanting to congratulate him and get their books signed and their pictures taken with the author. Her heart burst with love watching him, knowing that although he'd come to Marietta for all the wrong reasons, he'd stayed for all the right ones.

It was another hour before he joined her again, finding her in a rare quiet, alone moment, on the back porch, her forearms resting on the railing, champagne in hand, staring out at the leafy green orchard that had become Jude's pride and joy.

"Hey, you," he said, in that sexy undertone of his, nudging her with his shoulder as he, too, slid his forearms onto the railing beside hers, a bright red apple in each hand.

"Hey." She smiled. "You're a hit."

He grinned. "Let's hope it's a good omen for the sales to come."

"Amen to that," she said.

"You happy?" he asked, his peridot eyes searching hers.

Clem's chest tightened in a flood of emotion. "I didn't know it was possible to be this happy."

He smiled. "Neither did I." Then he handed her an apple. "A toast to us." He held it up like it was a glass. "To you and me and our forever."

Clem bumped her apple against his. "To our forever."

Then they raised them to their mouths and sealed their forever with two very satisfying crunches…

The End

Want more? Check out Vivian and Reuben's story in *All's Fair in Love and Chocolate*!

Join Tule Publishing's newsletter for more great reads and weekly deals!

Acknowledgements

I am indebted as always to the amazing women of Tule Publishing who work tirelessly behind the scenes to bring fabulous books to readers. To Jane, Meghan, Nikki, Cyndi and Sinclair – thank you, thank you. I once again bought this one in too close to the wire and your patience and reassurance was sincerely appreciated.

I'd also like to thank my daughter, Claire, who brainstormed this book with me one night on a very long mother-daughter road trip. It was fun sharing the process with her and letting her into the worlds inside my head. She might not be keen on reading her mother's books because *all that kissing, mum,* but she threw herself into the plotting of this story with enthusiasm and it was such a delight to see her getting so involved in Jude and Clementine's HEA. A few months ago, she left Australia for Ireland and a fresh new life with her lovely Irish lad. It brings me great joy that she is living her best life in a beautiful part of the world surrounded by people who love her as much as we do. Even if I do miss her every damn day.

Last but not least, thank you to my readers. Whether you've been with me for all my 80 plus books or I am just new to you – thank you. The way you love to read about love keeps me wanting to write about love. Here's to many more HEA's!

If you enjoyed *You Had Me at Chocolate,* you'll love the other book in the…

Marietta Chocolate Wars series

Book 1: *All's Fair in Love and Chocolate*

Book 2: *You Had Me at Chocolate*

Available now at your favorite online retailer!

More books by Amy Andrews

A Doctor for the Cowboy
American Extreme Bull Riders Tour series

Hot Mess
Hot Aussie Nights series

Seduced by the Baron
Fairy Tales of New York series

The Hero
Hot Aussie Heroes series

Outback Heat series

Welcome to Jumbuck Springs – a small, Aussie town in the midst of sheep country. They breed them tough in the outback, none more tough than the Weston family who have called Jumbuck Springs home for generations. Follow this smokin' hot series as all the Weston's find their HEA's in a blaze of outback heat.

Book 1: *Some Girls Do*

Book 2: *Some Girls Don't*

Book 3: *Some Guys Need a Lot of Lovin'*

Book 4: *Some Girls Lie*

Available now at your favorite online retailer!

About the Author

Amy Andrews is an award-winning, USA Today best-selling Aussie author who has written sixty plus contemporary romances in both the traditional and digital markets. She's sold two million books and been translated into over a dozen languages including manga. Her books bring all the feels from sass, quirk and laughter to emotional grit to panty-melting heat. Yes, her books feature lots of sex and kissing. You probably shouldn't try one if you think the sexy times belong behind closed doors – Amy rips the door right off the hinges.

She loves good books and great booze although she'll take mediocre booze if there's nothing else. She has two grown kids who have flown the coop for distant shores which is awesome because now she has a good reason to travel instead of because I want to.

At sixteen she met a guy she knew she was going to marry and she did. He's the kind of guy who can start a fire with nothing but two stones, construct a dwelling from half a dozen tree branches and a ball of string, mend anything that's broken with weird fixit juju and navigate home blindfolded with both arms tied behind his back but will also happily eat cornflakes for dinner when a deadline is looming. True hero material.

For many, many years she was a registered nurse. Which means she knows things. Anatomical things. And she's not afraid to use them!

She lives on acreage on the outskirts of Brisbane with a gorgeous mountain view but secretly wishes it was the hillsides of Tuscany.

Thank you for reading

You Had Me at Chocolate

If you enjoyed this book, you can find more from all our great authors at TulePublishing.com, or from your favorite online retailer.

Made in the USA
Coppell, TX
04 June 2024